THE
BRAHMIN
WARRIOR

R. Durgadoss is an entrepreneur, an inspirational speaker, a writer and a life coach. He holds a PhD in corporate governance and has had a career spanning more than three decades, with leading multinational institutions. He co-authored his first non-fiction bestseller, *A Saint in the Boardroom*, during his boardroom days. His deep-rooted passion for Indian mythology, history and philosophy pushed him to change his genre to the subjects that he loved most.

Having held audiences mesmerised with his powerful storytelling abilities during his corporate career, he decided to focus on a fiction series in the historical fiction genre. *The Shackles of the Warrior* was the first book in this series. Two more books followed—*The Indus Challenge* and *The Conquest of the East: Royal Crown Returns*. Given his passion to serve as a generator of hope for the youth, he now prefers to spend his time as a full-time author, and has now come out with the fourth book in the series, *The Brhamin Warrior*.

The author can be reached at:
https://m.facebook.com/DrDurgadoss/
He also has a website: http://www.drdd.co.in

Also by the author

The Indus Challenge
The Conquest of the East: Royal Crown Returns

THE
BRAHMIN
WARRIOR

R. DURGADOSS

RUPA

Published by
Rupa Publications India Pvt. Ltd 2019
7/16, Ansari Road, Daryaganj
New Delhi 110002

Sales centres:
Allahabad Bengaluru Chennai
Hyderabad Jaipur Kathmandu
Kolkata Mumbai

ISBN: 978-93-5333-692-9

First impression 2019

10 9 8 7 6 5 4 3 2 1

The moral right of the author has been asserted.

Printed by Nutech Print Services, Faridabad

To all the unsung heroes of medieval Bharat whom history has forgotten to recognize, record and revere

Contents

Introduction
Janam Four

Recap...
Track Travelled So Far...
Janam One: The Shackles of the Warrior

AD 2008

A terrorist group attacked the world by planting viruses into global computer systems through a satellite orbiting the earth. This act of cyberterrorism disrupted air traffic systems, interfered with the control systems for water and electricity, blocked commercial communications, caused various network systems to crash, compromised the confidentiality of military information and defaced websites. In light of this cyberattack, the world faced a chaotic situation.

Shiv, a young, celebrated NASA scientist, destroyed the group's moves and saved the earth from the cyberattacks. To honour Shiv's extraordinary performance, a felicitation function was held at the Taj Mahal Palace hotel, Mumbai, on the fateful day of 26 November 2008. Shiv, the cyberwarrior, fell prey to the terrorist attack at the Taj Mahal hotel. Several images flashed through his mind while he lay in a coma in the ICU of a leading hospital in Mumbai. The images of war, weapons and weeping widows swamped his mind. Were the flashes from his previous births?

The heroes who saved the planet from cyberterrorists could not avoid succumbing to physical terrorism. Shiv's unconscious mind questioned: Why?

The memories from his time in a coma were inexplicable. They were like a patchwork quilt, with no apparent sequence or temporal relationship with one another. The purest and most extraordinary part of his journey had commenced deep in his state of coma, whence his cerebrum unleashed a quest to unravel his past. Then, all of a sudden, everything opened up. His mind entered a valley whose beauty he could witness with clarity.

He could see waterfalls, lakes and indescribable hues of silver and gold, with rhythmic hymns emanating from them. Boom! Suddenly, the serene image disappeared and was replaced by images of war, weapons and weeping widows. He saw himself on the mast of a tall ship, in a missile silo, on the watchtower of a mammoth fort, and on a great warship, guiding its cannons. He then saw images of himself moving out of the earth and out of the universe. He lost awareness of his own physical body during his coma. During this search, his mind realized many of his previous states, breaking the shackles of the mysteries of his past lives.

His mind was filled with the chorus of a great army crying out the name, 'Sagar, Sagar, Sagar...' He was lying wounded on the battlefield, covered in deep cuts. There was bloodshed all around.

He was holding back his last breath, waiting for his beloved wife and newborn son. It was the battle between the Kauravas and the Pandavas, in the land situated between two rivers, the Sarasvati and the Drishadvati, the land where Manu wrote his *Manusmriti*, and the land where the *Rig* and *Sama* Vedas were compiled.

His calm mind resisted the image. 'This battleground is not my motherland or my beloved kingdom. This is not the place where

I spent my joyful childhood. This is not the beautiful place where I come from. I need to find the place of my birth.'

His comatose mind continued to wander further into the past. It now flashed images of the spectacular city of his birth. The golden fort of this city projected its yellow glitter on the surrounding waters, giving the impression of flames rising from the riverbed. There was a township with six sectors along the banks of the river. It was connected to the mainland via floating bridges, which could be withdrawn during invasions. The floating bridges and the design of the city were marvellous.

Having identified his motherland, he stumbled onto his colourful life as Sagar, the great warrior of the kingdom of Krishna in 3083 BC.

Sagar, in his first karmic avatar, was given the Shudra Varna tag but was patronized by a Brahmin guru. He was given the status of a Shudra by society but that of a strategic warrior by his leader, Abhimanyu.

Sagar grew up with three Brahmin friends, the sons of his Guruji, named Bharadwaj, the Kshatriya leader Abhimanyu, and another friend who was a Vaishya. A close bond developed among them at the gurukul.

The three sons of his Guruji were blessed with mystic powers. All the Pancha bhoodas—earth, water, sky, air and fire—danced to the tunes of the three boys who were born as triplets. All of them were more or less the same age as Sagar.

One boy was extraordinarily proficient in matters concerning the earth. He knew the topography, water bodies, when an earthquake was likely to happen and ways to create tremors in the earth. He could identify the movement of creatures beneath the ground. He could create a hole, go into the earth and come out of another place by navigating the surface below. He could stay beneath the earth for months without anyone's knowledge. When he fought on earth, no one could conquer him.

The second boy was blessed with extraordinary powers under water. He could swim under water, stay under it for ages, invoke Varuna and summon rain at will. When he fought on water, he was invincible.

The third boy was highly talented in matters of the sky. He could invoke Vayu, change the direction of the wind, speak to birds and communicate with people in far-off places through the air. When he fought from a height, no one could defeat him.

But the Pancha bhoodas would only obey them when the three of them were together. They were warned of a threat that would befall them at the age of fifteen. As they grew older, they joined Abhimanyu's 'Yuva Warrior' team.

Sagar was the chief strategist of the Yuva Sena, marshalling resources for his leader Abhimanyu. During the Kurukshetra War, on the fateful day of the chakravyuha, Sagar had been advised by his Guruji that he should not send his three gifted sons to the field. According to their horoscopes, their lives were under threat.

But fate took the decision away from him.

A nine-layer chakravyuha had been formed by Guru Drona. All of Duryodhana's greatest warriors were in the inner circle while the outer circle was protected by the mighty Drona. The Pandava warrior Arjuna, the only one who knew how to cleave the chakravyuha, had been dragged off to a different field. Now, the onus of breaking the chakravyuha fell upon the young Abhimanyu, Arjuna's son. He knew how to break into the chakravyuha, but he did not know how to exit.

The Yuva Sena, headed by Abhimanyu, volunteered to enter the chakravyuha, assigning the seniors the task of ensuring that the breach remained open, to allow for a clear line of retreat. A contingency plan was made.

↑
Chakravyuha Entrance

The three Brahmin boys' powers would be used to create an underground tunnel through each tier, so that the soldiers would be able to retreat in case of any mishaps. A portion of the army could also use the tunnels so that they could be shielded from arrows while moving ahead and defending the broken edges of the tier. Also, even if the tiers were closed due to any reason, the mouths of the tunnels would provide a ready exit for Abhimanyu.

The innovative tactic of outsmarting the chakravyuha by using the mystical powers of the Sena brothers was deliberated upon in the strategy discussions, held during the early meetings.

When the Yuva Sena was ready to enter the chakravyuha, one of the southern kings supporting the Pandavas thundered: 'How do you expect my forces to be led by a Shudra? It's not possible. I will not allow this.'

Abhimanyu and Sagar were hurt. They knew that time was being wasted. The arrangement of forces to counter the chakravyuha would take at least half a nazhigai. One nazhigai equals twenty-four minutes, and a day is divided into 60 nazhigais. Abhimanyu asked Sagar to stay silent and stated that he would explain the situation. But no one was listening to him. As the talks were on between Abhimanyu and the southern kings, an emissary arrived with a message, stating that Sagar's wife, Varsha, had given birth to a baby boy.

Abhimanyu wanted Sagar to visit his wife, see his son and come back. In the meantime, he would make the arrangements for the army. But the southern kings were adamant. They would not fight under a Shudra. Exasperated, Abhimanyu and Sagar gave up. Abhimanyu instructed Sagar to go back and be with his wife. He asked one of the southern kings to be the rear guard instead.

Sagar said to Abhimanyu, 'I do not know whether to be happy for my son or sad that on the eve of battle, I cannot be with you.'

Abhimanyu replied, 'Keep the sweets ready. I will come back and we will celebrate the birth of your son.'

Sagar went to his Brahmin friends and said, 'You should be very careful. Stay with Abhimanyu at all times. As long as you are with Abhimanyu, I will not be afraid. Also, under no circumstances should you get separated. Stay together and ride together.'

Sagar moved off the battlefield with a feeling of guilt, afraid that he was leaving the three boys and foregoing his Guruji's strict instructions.

In the meantime, Abhimanyu's young blood and the heat of the battle overtook him. He fought like a warrior who does not value his own life. He started to move further ahead while his army, which could not match his swiftness, began to fall back. All his uncles were stuck far behind near the first tier of the chakravyuha.

His rear guard was pursued and attacked by Drona. The three

Brahmin boys with special powers were separated in the melee that took place. Since they were separated, they could not invoke the Pancha bhoodas, as their mystic skills only worked when they were together. Plans for the tunnel were turned to dust, and with them went the last ray of hope for a safe return.

Moreover, the strategy master, Sagar, who channelized the mystic powers of the Brahmin boys into a coordinated strategy, was not with them. Hence, each one of them became a powerless island, lending no assistance with their supernatural abilities.

The senior Pandavas were held back at the entrance of the chakravyuha while the circles of the chakravyuha were closed by their opponents, leaving the Yuva Sena warriors—Abhimanyu and the three Brahmin boys—stuck inside different tiers. After a valiant battle, the soul of the young hero Abhimanyu departed this world, unsatisfied. He had fought bravely, to the best of his abilities. Had his opponents been honourable, and had he got more time, he would surely have destroyed all of them. Drona was satisfied, as he had struck a blow that would hurt the Pandavas. The chakravyuha had served its purpose.

Among the thousands who died that day were the three Brahmin boys. Not being able to evoke their mystical powers, they lay dead in different tiers within the chakravyuha.

Sagar had been betrayed by his Vaishya wife. She had married him, pretending to love him, while in fact she desired to take revenge on him thinking that his Shudra father had been the cause of her father's death. She had unveiled their secret plan for the chakravyuha to the enemy, which wreaked havoc on the Yuva Sena warriors—including Abimanyu and the three Brahmin boys.

Sagar spoke of the tragedy to his Guruji, who was meditating across the river. He roared, 'Sagar, I told you not to send my three sons to the war, as they faced a life threat at the age of fifteen. You promised to protect them. You are responsible for this.

You knew they were blessed children. They were supposed to be extraordinary warriors on land, sea and air, supported by all the Pancha bhoodas. You shortened their lives. They might have lived at least three times longer. The story of their lives will always be one of success, and incompleteness. You have nipped their lives in the bud by not sticking to your word.

'I hereby curse you. You will live the forty-five years of each of my sons' remaining lives. But you will not live them in full. You will have the capability of each of my sons, and like them, you will also die at the age of fifteen. Thus, you will take three births for each of my sons. You will take nine incarnations after this birth.'

'You will be highly competent on land, sea and air in each of the three births. You might win a war, but you cannot avail the fruits of it. Let these nine births forever remind you that you killed my sons in the nine-tier chakravyuha. Each of the nine circles will represent one birth for you. This is my curse. And yet, my anger is not slaked.'

Sagar was stunned. He could not understand how quickly his fate had turned around. His guru, the one who had almost adopted him, who was equal to his own father and had been everything to him, had turned against him.

'He is a true Brahmin, and his curse will force me to face miseries in my subsequent births,' he thought.

He pleaded with his guru, saying that he was not the only cause behind the death of his sons. He explained how circumstances such as the birth of his son and the revolt of the southern kings had prohibited him from participating in the battle that day. But Guruji did not reply to him, did not bother to listen to him, and turned away.

Later, as he lay on his deathbed the next day, Sagar learned the secrets of his birth in a Kshatriya family and also about the betrayal of his wife.

He pleaded with his Guruji on his deathbed.

'Guruji, I was penalized as a low-caste Shudra, even though I was born a Kshatriya. I was penalized by my wife for a cause to which my family and I were not party. I was penalized by you for the death of your sons for which I was not the cause.

'I do not know why I have been singled out by my fate and punished for no fault of mine. But I will not curse my fate; I lived true to the people around me, I was passionate in whatever I was doing, and I am willing to accept the results as they unfold. I truly believe that I have had to chase my goals, but at the same time, I have had to learn to face the results. My only wish is that no one on earth be denied opportunities on grounds of his caste, creed or colour.

'Life may crown a person or make him a beggar on the streets. But no one should deprive anyone else of opportunities. Everyone should have equal opportunities. From below the ground comes a diamond, from the mud comes the lotus. Greatness can come from anyone. A mother's womb should not determine one's destiny. I am saying this after facing troubles from the womb to my tomb. This is my death wish, Guruji,' Sagar concluded.

Bharadwaj had tears in his eyes. 'My dear Sagar, you speak like a philosopher. You have matured beyond your age. In the philosophy sessions at the gurukul, I saw the sparks in you. Today, I am seeing those sparks become flames. I have to correct myself. I cursed you with short lives in your nine future births.

'I cannot take back my curse, and the arrow once out of the bow cannot be retrieved. I have no power to withdraw it, but I can soften the curse. For each of the nine births to follow, I double your years from fifteen to thirty. That is the best I can do, Sagar. But in every one of your births, you will have a great impact on society. In three of your births, you will have special powers regarding land. In the following three, you will have special powers over water and in the last three, you will have special powers over air. Had my sons lived, they would have excelled in land, water and air.'

Turning to Sagar's wife, Bharadwaj said, 'You lived a false life with Sagar, even though he gave you pure love. For cheating on him like this, you will continuously beg for his help as a prisoner of war in your next birth. You will meet your husband, who will be the army chief, and save you from prison. You have the chance to break your own chakras of rebirth if you sincerely love your husband in the next birth.'

A new journey was about to begin for these two souls. The soul of Varsha would next be a prisoner of war, begging and pleading for support from the soul of Sagar. Where would this meeting take place? What sort of people would they be in their next outing?

The Indus Challenge: Janam Two

Sagar was reborn as Rudra in janam two in 330 BC. It was at this time that the people of Bharat were looking inwards, while the Macedonians, led by Alexander the Great, aggressively spread outwards and wanted to conquer the world. The kingdoms of Bharat were also threatened. In the second avatar, janam two of Rudra, during the tumultuous times of Alexander and Chanakya, he offered stunning clues and left a trail that answered many mysteries in our rich history. Rudra, heading the Nine Unknown Men (NUM) Army, decoded the secrets to save humanity from cataclysm and extinction.

Rudra fought against the treachery of the enemies from within and saved his Maurya emperor and his kingdom from plunging into chaos.

Rudra, the man who protected his emperor and his sons, was killed by poison mixed with sacred water at a temple. The same sacred water that killed him welcomed him at his birth in his next karmic outing, talked about in *The Conquest of the East: Royal Crown Returns* in his janam three.

The Conquest of the East: Janam Three

The domination of the Cholas started with the efforts of Rajaraja Chola, who grew his kingdom and military strength from his capital city of Thanjavur in Tamil Nadu. The enemies could not bear his onslaught, yet, he could not complete one agenda, which forever eluded his success. His grandfather had won the war against the Pandyas but could not declare it a real triumph. The Pandyan king fled with the coveted 'royal crown', the mythical aaram (a neckpiece) and a precious garland, leaving everything in the custody of the Lankan king.

Rajaraja Chola tried to restore his kingdom's pride by capturing these regal jewels from the Lankans. Yet again, he could win the war but could not finish it as an emphatic victory. This time, it was the Lankan king who managed to flee with the Pandya's regal jewels. Ultimately, Rajaraja Chola had to leave this task to his son Rajendra Chola.

In his third avatar as Surya, during this challenging time of Rajaraja and Rajendra Chola, he showed an unbreakable spirit by taking this massive task upon himself. Ultimately, he gave up his life, saving his emperor and safeguarding his empire from the enemies.

The great warrior Surya, who was killed by a Vedic Brahmin pandit, was reborn in a similar Brahmin family as Aditya, in 1528, supporting Hemu, the Hindu warrior fighting the Mughals.

Would he be able to break the shackles of destiny and overcome the curse in his new avatar as Aditya?

Prologue

The invaders—Turks, Persians, Arabs, Mongolians and Afghans—were raiding the kingdoms of Bharat. Since AD 1290, the Afghans had been ruling the Delhi Sultanate under Ibrahim Lodi when he met Babur in the First Battle of Panipat in 1526. During that time, the important provinces of Oudh, Jaunpur and western Bihar revolted against Ibrahim Lodi. Bengal under its king Nasiruddin Nasrat Shah, Gujarat under Sikandar Shah and Malwa under Sultan Mahmud were three powerful kingdoms. A portion of Malwa, represented by the fortresses of Ranthambore, Sarangpur, Bhilsa, Chanderi and Chittor, were re-conquered by the Hindu prince Rana Sanga. In south India, the Bahmanis had established their kingdom. The raja of Vijayanagar exercised independent authority. A considerable number of rajas never submitted to Islamic kings.

It was a dazzling period of Islam from the invaders' point of view. They had the immense satisfaction of sending millions of accursed kafirs to hell in a continuous war, demolishing and desecrating thousands of idolatrous places of worship and pilgrimage, killing thousands of Brahmins and bhikshus, forcing people to eat beef, collecting vast amounts of bounty which they distributed amongst themselves, capturing millions of men, women and children and selling them into slavery and concubinage in far-off countries ranging from Kabul to Persia, and usurping power and privilege over a vast population which was reduced to serfdom by the power of the sword.

Bharat in 1524 before Babur's conquest of the Delhi Sultanate

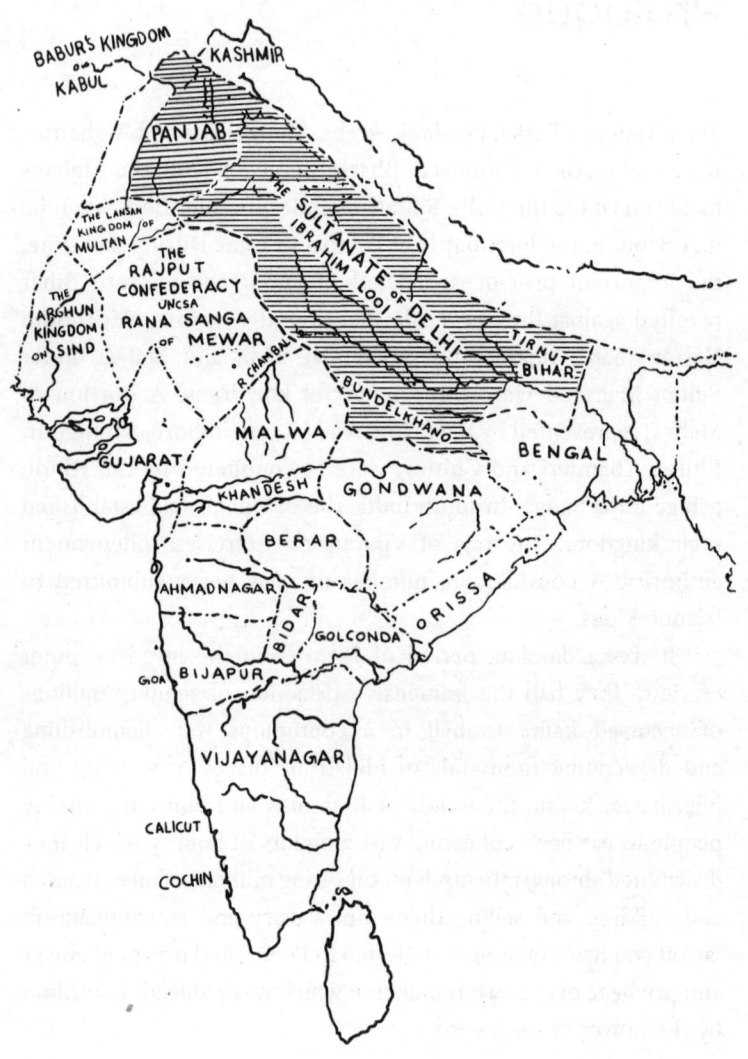

For the Hindus, this period was a prolonged spell of darkness. Their idols were mutilated or melted down, stone idols were broken and used as steps in mosques, Brahmin priests were molested or arrested, temples were damaged or converted into mosques and cows were slaughtered on temple sites to prevent Hindus from visiting them again. The invaders destroyed Hindu holy scriptures, conch shells and articles of worship. They draped their bodies in sandalwood paste and licked it off to hurt Hindu sentiments. Tulsi plants were uprooted and bathing in the Ganges was prohibited. The invaders even spat in the mouths of Brahmin priests. Innumerable taxes, including pilgrimage tax, trade tax, tax for toleration (zar-i-zimmiya) and tax for pursuing Hinduism (jizya) were to be paid by Hindus. The situation was so harsh that if a revenue officer spat into the mouth of a Hindu tax defaulter, the latter could not protest. If people defaulted in tax payments, their wives and children had to be sold as slaves.

Hindu women suffered greatly. Once a war was won, the daughters of the captured infidel rajas would be given to ameers. The daughters of the other infidels would be given to the sultan's relatives. The other captured women infidels would be sold as slaves. The Rajputra king had to leave one male child with the sultan to serve as prisoner of war. Similarly, the rajas had to marry off their daughters to the sultan. Many Hindu names of people and places were changed to Islamic ones.

Mass conversions by force and the violation of the chastity of Hindu women were very common. The invaders could rule the country only through systemic terror. Cruelty was the norm: burnings, executions, crucifixions or impalements, and other inventive tortures, took place regularly. If ever there was an uprising, it was instantly and savagely repressed. The countryside was plundered, men were slaughtered and women were enslaved.

During this time, Babur conquered Delhi in the First Battle

of Panipat in 1526, defeating Ibrahim Lodi. With his superior generalship and military techniques, and an excellent cavalry and artillery, Babur quickly took over the vast empire.

Thus, Babur announced his arrival in Hindustan. With the next battle with Rana Sanga at Khanwa, he loudly announced his intention of ruling the whole of Hindustan. After this victory, he directed that a tower of heads was to be erected on a raised ground near his camp. Here, the noblest heads of Rajputana, the land of Hindu Rajput warriors, were heaped in a ghastly pyramid. He proclaimed his victory by assuming the title of 'Ghazi'—a victor in a holy war against kafirs, the slayer of infidels. The battleground flowed with so much blood and became so full of quivering carcasses that his tent had to be moved thrice, to a higher level. He lost no opportunity to capture prisoners of war and assume plunder.

Yet, the Rajputs were not completely shattered. They were trying to regroup under the proud Medini Rai, one of the trusted lieutenants of Rana Sanga who escaped from the Battle of Khanwa. He was well entrenched in the famous fortress of Chanderi, situated on the eastern edge of Rajasthan, with 5,000 Rajput warriors.

Babur reached Chanderi Fort on 21 January 1528. The Battle of Chanderi had just begun.

PART I

....

The Siege of Chanderi Fort

1

The fort was located on a hill southwest of the river Betwa. It was situated strategically on the border between Malwa and Bundelkhand, surrounded by hills, lakes and forests. There were several sandstone hills on all sides. Andhyari Pahari, Gurela Pahari, Salia Pahari, Mungra Pahari, Manjera Pahari, Gol Pahari, Chandela Pahari and many other such hills extended natural protection, making it an impregnable fort.

The forests were blessed with fruit trees: aam, imli, jamun, khajur, mahua and many more. Apart from these, tall teak trees added to their grandeur. The sounds of leopards, bears, wild dogs and wild cats frightened the incumbent troops of Babur, who were new to the terrain.

The dark night with the glittering moon justified the name Chandragiri, the mountain of Chanderi. Chanderi has an ancient origin and finds reference in the *Mahabharata* as a Chedi country ruled by Shishu Pala, the cousin of Lord Krishna. Subsequently, the Chanderi township was set up by Kirtipal, a king of the Pratihara lineage in the eleventh century. It was then ruled by the Kachwa Rajputs. Then came Balban, a minister of Sultan Nasiruddin of Delhi, who captured Chanderi from the Rajputs in the thirteenth century. It was subsequently annexed by Alauddin Khalji.

In the fourteenth century, the town became a sprawling city full of bazaars thronged by people and goods. Its proximity to the trade routes of Central India, Malwa and Mewar made it popular. In the fifteenth century, Chanderi was incorporated into the Malwa Sultanate. Hardly eight years ago, Rana Sanga, the Rajput king, had captured Chanderi and bestowed it on the current ruler, Medini Rai.

Babur was briefed by Raja Silhadi, who had recently betrayed Rana Sanga and switched sides in the just-concluded battle of Khanwa.

'Interesting, Silhadi, Chanderi Fort has a great history behind it,' Babur exclaimed. He started taking strategic inputs about the Rajput confederation from Raja Silhadi, who had once been a key lieutenant of Rana Sanga along with Medini Rai.

Raja Silhadi was promised by Babur that his territory would not be attacked if he betrayed Rana Sanga.

'Your Majesty, Chanderi is an important military outpost for many ruling kingdoms in this region. Chanderi Fort dominates the skyline of the lovely town of Chanderi. The fort is situated on Chandragiri hill, 250 feet above the town. The citadel's water supply is lower down the hill and is protected by a double line of walls that run from the citadel to the outer fort. The main gate of the town is known as Khooni Darwaja. It has been named so because criminals were thrown from the battlements above, and their bodies were crushed to death below. The fortifying walls were constructed by the sultan of Malwa. To the southwest of the fort is a mysterious gateway called "katti-gatti" which passes through the hills. The walls are so strong, even our cannons cannot destroy them easily.'

'We will find other ways,' quipped Babur. 'The water from the springs is very tasty, Silhadi.'

'Yes, Your Majesty, the springs have a story behind them. A king of the eleventh century, Kirtipal of the Prathihara dynasty, was cured of leprosy by the waters of a spring that he chanced upon during a hunting expedition. That is why it is called "the miraculous water". The king moved his palace to this place and constructed three entities: Kirti Durg, Kirti Narayana and Kirti Sagar. Kirti Sagar contains the water from the spring. Kirti Narayana is a Vaishnav temple built inside the fort. The presiding deity, Vishnu, is made of gold. The adjoining deities are made of precious emerald stones. It is said that beneath the deities are placed precious jewels and gold ornaments,' Silhadi continued.

'That means our men will have a lot of work inside the fort, won't they, Silhadi?' Babur intervened.

'The fort has a masjid inside, built by the sultan of Malwa, Your Majesty. There is a beautiful three-storeyed palace inside the fort, with a fountain and a tank in its courtyard and bastions and watch towers in the corners. Medini Rai has assembled all the nobles and army men here, for a few royal weddings in the palace. All the royal members of the Rajput families have assembled here. Vedic pandits from different parts of the kingdom have come here to perform rituals. They have no clue about Your Majesty's arrival here.'

'Well, we will spring a surprise on them, Silhadi! Tell me more about Medini Rai. Who is he?' Babur asked pointedly.

∽

2

'The Malwa Sultanate was assisted by Medini Rai and Silhadi, two Hindu Rajput generals. The two revolted against Mehmud Khilji, the ruler of Malwa. The sultan had to seek the assistance of Ibrahim Lodi, the sultan of Delhi, and Bahadur Shah of Gujarat.

'Meanwhile, Medini Rai and Silhadi, the Rajput rebels, sought the help of Rana Sanga, the Rajput king who was expanding his Rajput confederate. They defeated the sultan of Malwa and took over control. This emboldened Rana Sanga to wage subsequent wars against Ibrahim Lodi.

'Despite being badly injured in these wars, Rana Sanga captured several areas, including the fort of Ranthambore. He defeated Ibrahim Lodi in the battles of Khatoli and Dholapur, but he lost his left arm and was crippled in one leg. Following these battles, Rana Sanga became a principal player in North India.

'Medini Rai was just a small warlord before those battles, but he contributed everything in his power for which he was rewarded by Rana Sanga. Chanderi, which fell into the hands of Rana Sanga, was bestowed upon Medini Rai. That is how he became the ruler of Chanderi,' Mustafa Rumi, the senior commander of Babur, narrated the story of Medini Rai.

'That means Medini Rai was your partner, Silhadi?' Babur asked Silhadi who was sitting next to him.

'Yes, he once was. But he was rewarded with Chanderi. I was not blessed with such royal gifts, Your Majesty.'

'That is why you ditched Rana Sanga in the battle of Khanwa, with all your five thousand soldiers...'

'Yes, Your Majesty. I accompanied him in the battle, but at a crucial point I turned against him. He never expected his own lieutenant to wage a war against him and join his enemy, the Badshah Babur, Your Majesty.'

'Silhadi, you did provide me with great support. I will remember your help all my life. I will never attack your territory, my friend. By the way, did you call me Badshah? Wait, until I conquer Chanderi Fort, I will not take that title, Silhadi. Tell me, wasn't Medini Rai a pet commander of the sultan of Malwa? Why did he revolt against him?'

'Yes, he was once the favourite minister of Mahmud Shah bin Nasir Shah, Sultan of Malwa. But during one of the conquests, he forcibly took away Muslim women and made them his slaves and dance girls. He was ordered to free the women and seek their forgiveness. This incident created a rift between him and the sultan, leading to his dismissal. Ultimately, he joined Rana Sanga to defeat the sultan of Malwa.'

'What? He had the courage to make our Muslim women his slaves? We will teach him a lesson here at his very own citadel!' Babur thundered. 'Let me assess our preparedness and convene a meeting of our commanders.'

∞

3

Babur's camp was in full attendance. Humayun, the crown prince, and the commanders Ustad Ali Quli, Mustafa Rumi, Timur Khan, Muhammed Ali Khan, Askari Mirza and Raja Silhadi were all present.

'My comrades, have you assessed the strength of our enemy inside Chanderi Fort?' Babur took the chair.

'Your Majesty, our spies have been receiving conflicting information. Some inputs state that Medini Rai is caught unawares. He is busy with the royal vivah that is being conducted inside the fort. He has called all his nobles, and a grand ceremony is being hosted inside the fort. There is an atmosphere of festivity inside; they are not aware of the siege yet.

'But some other sources reveal that the fort is well guarded by about five thousand Rajput warriors who are fierce fighters. Because he is guarded by such loyal and fierce fighters, Medini Rai is not bothered by any possibility of siege of his fort. He is not perturbed at all. We do not know which sources are correct,' said Askari Mirza, the spy chief.

'Silhadi, you were once the comrade of Medini Rai. You know the tricks of his trade. What is your assessment of this situation?' Babur looked at Silhadi.

'Your Majesty, Medini Rai and his fierce fighters cannot be underestimated. About five to six thousand of his men escaped from the battle of Khanwa, where Rana Sanga was defeated by us. Medini Rai is a tactician; he may plant false news to deceive us. He might have planted a false story about his unpreparedness. We should not take him lightly, Your Majesty.'

'You say that he is deceiving us.'

'Yes, Your Majesty. He must have at least eight to ten thousand men with him.'

'Oh, we also have about seven thousand and five hundred men and the support of the cannons with us.'

'No, Your Majesty. Medini Rai has counter cannon attack capability installed on top of his fort. He has procured guns from China and Gujarat through his trade channels headed by Hemu, the gun trader who also used to supply to Ibrahim Lodi.'

'Is that so? I thought Hindustani rulers lacked the exposure to guns and gunpowder.'

'You are mistaken, Your Majesty. Details about guns called *agnichurna*, used in ancient Hindustan, are found in the Shukra Niti. Similar weapons find mention in the *Atharva Veda*. Information about cannons is found in the *Mahabharata*. They were called *shatagni* in ancient Hindustan. A shatagni had the capacity to kill nearly a hundred soldiers at a time. It was a large gun that used to fire iron balls fitted with spikes. It was mounted on a vehicle that had eight wheels. There were guns known as *bhusundi* in ancient Hindustan. Small guns were known as *laghu naliyam* and the bigger ones were known as *briha naliyam*.'

'Silhadi, now you have started bragging about your ancient

past. All of you live in a mythological past for which you have no evidence. Experimenting with life-lengthening elixirs, a Chinese alchemist ended up discovering gunpowder. Ironically, it was the quest for immortality that led to the invention of the deadliest gunpowder weapon. This explosive invention formed the basis of almost every weapon used in war, from fiery arrows to rifles, cannons and grenades. Our Mongol ancestors were the first to face this flying fire: an arrow fixed with a tube of gunpowder that ignited and propelled itself across enemy lines. Later, the creation of a large united Mongol empire resulted in the free transmission of Chinese technology into parts of Hindustan that had been conquered by the Mongols. That is how the Delhi Sultanate as well as the Bahmani kingdom in the south made good use of them.'

'Firearms are also used by the Vijayanagar empire, Your Majesty.'

'Silhadi, we have made considerable changes in the way we use cannons and guns in Hindustan, using light-weight carts as carriers. Anyway, let me ask my cannon squad head, Ustad Ali.'

'Ali, how long will you take to break the tall walls of Chanderi Fort?'

'Your Majesty, I have surveyed them. The walls are so strong that we will need considerable time to break them.'

'What? Can't you break the walls in two days? Then I will ask my soldiers to climb up the walls and enter the fort from the top.'

While the discussions were on, a sudden message brought by a messenger shook the whole camp.

4

Babur's minister Mir Khalifa rushed in. He was in great panic. 'Your Majesty, our troops appointed to the east have been defeated and have come back to Kanauj. They are awaiting your instructions. We need to go to Kanauj, leaving Chanderi's siege for now!'

Babur listened to him calmly. Retaining his composure, he said, 'Mir Khalifa, it is useless to be worried and upset. Whatever is written in our fortune will happen. We should not think about what we heard just now. Tomorrow, we should deliver our assault here at Chanderi. We need to finish this Rajput ruler, otherwise he will become a great nuisance for us.'

'But we have only five thousand men, Your Majesty. We learn from some sources that Medini Rai is well-armed, with a sufficient number of men inside,' Mir Khalifa interjected.

'We are not clear about the exact strength of Medini Rai's forces inside the fort. You do one thing. Just hold back the news of our defeat in the east from our men here at Chanderi. Let them not get demoralized. Anyway, we will play it safe here.

'Let me propose three options for Medini Rai: first, he and his court can leave Chanderi unmolested and concede it to us. Second, Medini Rai and his court can surrender to us. He can be the king, but under the rule of Babur. He can be given a new territory, Shamsabad, if he accepts this. And third, Medini Rai does not accept our terms, and we attack. These are the three options we can give Medini Rai.'

'But who will carry the message, Your Majesty? The person carrying the message cannot even enter the fort,' Mir Khalifa asked.

'Don't worry; we will deliver these messages through the

people of the town. Our forces camped outside the town can pass on the message through the people of the town living on the fringes of the fort.'

Meanwhile, inside Chanderi Fort, there was festivity all around and people were completely oblivious to the developments outside.

⌘

5

The palace wore a festive look, well illuminated all around. It was witnessing royal vivah celebrations. There were about a thousand nobles, aristocrats and members of the royal family. All of them were dressed well. The well-decorated venue, colourful outfits and delicious food testified to the grandeur of the wedding.

There were two functions scheduled for the day. The first one was the Nischaya Mahotsav or engagement ceremony, followed by the day-long vivah.

Medini Rai had twin daughters, Sainthavi and Sambhavi. Both the beautiful princesses were getting engaged to Ratan Singh and Vikramaditya Singh respectively, the sons of Rana Sanga of Mewar.

Rana Sanga wanted to cement his relationship with Medini Rai, who was very loyal to him. Medini Rai was yet to recover from the shock of defeat at the Battle of Khanwa. His minister, Harsha Rai, tried to make conversation with him.

'Your Majesty, we have to go ahead with the function, even though Rana Sanga is not amidst us today.'

'Yes, Harsha, that is what I was thinking about. Luckily, Rana Sanga is safe and is now resting at an undisclosed destination. He was badly wounded in the battle. But before leaving the battlefield, he asked me to retreat and lie low for some time. He said that we could recoup our forces and come back stronger. But he wanted me to go ahead with the functions at Chanderi Fort, as it is far away from Khanwa. As this is a safe location, away from the enemy, I called all our nobles and royal family members here to celebrate in a grand manner; of course, under the advice of Rana Sanga himself!'

As he spoke, the engagement ceremony commenced.

The bridegrooms, Ratan Singh and Vikramaditya Singh, were ready. Wearing diamond-studded sherwanis and family turbans, each wielding a sword in his left hand, they oozed royalty from every one of their movements.

The brides, Sainthavi and Sambhavi, wore glittering bridal dresses with beautiful embroidery. Each was adorned with a *rakhdi* on her forehead, a *baju* above her elbows, diamond necklaces, *poonchis* and *bangdis* on her hands and *pajebs* around her ankles, perfectly complementing her ravishing beauty.

The palace head priest, Bhargav Ram, was busy performing the Vedic rituals.

The families of both the brides and the grooms were present, attired in their best. Rana Sanga's queen, Rani Karnavati, was heading their family in the absence of her husband.

Medini Rai was heading the brides' family. Bhargav Ram read out the Patra Lagnam Patrika.

'Om Shri Namo Narayana! On this auspicious day, the third day of the Magha month, the maharaja of Mewar, Rana Sanga, and the Raja of Chanderi, Medini Rai, agree to enter into a vivah alliance. The first daughter of Medini Rai, Sainthavi, will wed Ratan Singh, the first son of Maharaja Rana Sanga. The second daughter of Medini Rai, Sambhavi, will wed Vikramaditya Singh, the second son of Rana Sanga. The vivah will take place on the Mithuna lagna, on the sixth day of the Magha month.'

All the people assembled applauded, and both the families

exchanged the patrika on a plate loaded with fruits, flowers and gifts. Both families symbolically agreed to support each other and share the good and the bad. With this, the first function was over.

Then the next function, a vivah, started. Arjun was the bridegroom. He was Medini Rai's nephew. Medini Rai was very attached to his eldest sister. She had brought him up as a young boy, since his mother had passed away giving birth to him. Medini Rai did not have a son; he only had two daughters. He had groomed Arjun as his heir apparent.

Arjun loved Heera. Heera was the daughter of Meera and Bhargav Ram, the head priest. Meera was from the Vaishya community of Rewari. She was the sister of Hemchandra, or Hemu, the up-and-coming trader. Bhargav Ram belonged to a Brahmin priestly family of Rewari. Both loved each other. They had got married, walking away from their families who vehemently opposed their inter-caste marriage. Their beautiful sixteen-year-old daughter Heera loved Arjun, the Kshatriya Rajput warrior. Since Bhargav Ram was the head priest of Chanderi Palace, Medini Rai did not object to this marriage. A girl born of the union of a Vaishya and a Brahmin was marrying a Rajput Kshatriya boy from a royal family. Their marriage was lavishly celebrated that day.

6

The day-long celebrations were on in full swing. Marriage is a relationship that lasts for seven lives, between the families of the bride and the groom. It comprises of a series of ceremonies: a function for the tilak or engagement; the *ban* or commencement of the wedding ceremony; the *mel* or community feast; the *nikasi* or departure of the bridegroom's party for the wedding; the *sehla* and the *dhukav* or the reception hosted by the bride's parents.

Finally, the most important ceremony of the day, the *mangal phera*, took place. The couple walked around the sacred fire to affirm their marriage. Offerings of ghee and sesame seeds were poured into the sacred fire while the chanting of mantras filled the air.

The priest chanted prayers to the stars, planets, moon, sun and Vishnu the preserver, which the groom repeated after him. Prayers were then offered by the bride to Yama, the God of death, seeking a long life for the groom.

The first *phera* or circumambulation around the fire is for *dharma*, the basic principles of day to day life. This is initiated by the bride's family.

The second *phera* is for understanding the meaning of the religious life of earthly professions under the umbrella of Hindu dharma.

The third *phera* is to ensure karma and to promise that the couple will teach their children the principles and values of Hindu dharma.

The fourth *phera* is for moksha, the promise that when the couple has fulfilled their life's material goals, they will lead the lives of hermits and free themselves from worldly desires.

During these seven *pheras*, prayers included requests for plentiful, nourishing and pure food, a healthy and prosperous life, spiritual and mental health, wealth, sharing happiness and pain together, increase in love and respect for each other and each other's families, birth of heroic and noble children, a peaceful life with each other, companionship, togetherness, loyalty and understanding between themselves.

After the seven *pheras*, Arjun the groom said to his wife Heera that they had now become friends and that they would remain so throughout their lives.

Next was the most important part of the vivah, the *mangalya dharanam*.

Bhargav Ram, the head priest, was reciting the Vedic mantra himself for his daughter's marriage, with his wife sitting next to him. She was in an advanced stage of pregnancy, due to deliver any time. They were having a second child after sixteen years, but the couple did not want the delivery to delay the wedding of their daughter. That was because Medini Rai wanted to complete the wedding on this auspicious day, as he had to proceed with the war preparations quickly, post the defeat at the hands of Babur in the Battle of Khanwa.

Along with Bhargav Ram, the deputy priest Keshav Ram recited the following mantra loudly on behalf of the groom:

Mangalyam tantunanena mama jeevana hetunah
kanthe badhnami subhage twam jeeva sarada satam

The bridegroom, through this mantra, declared his intention of tying the mangalyam around his bride's neck: 'As a token of remembrance for our future lives, I am tying this mangalsutra around your neck. May you enjoy your married life for a hundred years.'

A chain made with a set of black beads attached to a gold pendant was the sacred mangalyam uniting the groom and bride for life. Tears of joy rolled down the faces of Heera's parents. They had been completely denounced by both their families after their wedding, since theirs had been an inter-caste marriage. Both of them had walked away from their families and been married in a temple, with no celebrations for them. Hence, this royal wedding of their daughter brought tears of joy to their eyes.

Then, there was a feast hosted by Medini Rai for the invitees. The cuisine comprised delicious vegetarian dishes, since this was the wedding of a Brahmin priest's daughter. There were some Vaishnavas who were also strict vegetarians, for whom delicious dal baati was served. *Dal baati* is a dish of cooked lentils and roasted balls of dough, served along with a number of dried or pickled berries cooked in different ways.

Finally, the *indra pravesh* ceremony took place. This function marks the entry of the bride into her husband's house for the first time. The bride arrived at her father-in-law's house. Games were played between the bride and the groom. There was an air of happiness all around.

The celebrations finally ended with the *suhag raat* for the couple. For this, one of the rooms of the palace was decorated with fragrant and fresh rajnigandha and jasmine flowers. It is believed that the sweet natural fragrance of the flowers creates a romantic mood for couples to begin this new chapter in their lives.

Arjun was delayed by the barricades made by his sisters. They asked him for a heavy 'through fare' to access the decorated room. Arjun had to negotiate with them and placate them with many gifts before gaining entry into the decorated room.

Heera was dressed in her bridal attire, a ghunghat or veil covering her face. She was waiting for him to unveil her.

Leaving the couple in the room, all the relatives went to their rooms to rest.

The *suhag raat* started for the couple.

7

Arjun walked in. The couple had known each other for long; they had spent long hours as lovers, talking about many things. But the bride naturally feels shy on the *suhag raat*.

'Welcome, Heera,' Arjun said, giving her a gift, asking her to unwrap the package.

Heera excitedly opened it. It was a beautiful Ardhanareeswara statue made of gold.

The figure symbolizes that the male and female principles are inseparable. The composite form conveys the unity of opposites in the universe.

'What a beautiful statue! Why a Shiva-Shakti statue for this Vaishnav girl?' Heera smilingly posed her question.

'You are always within me, Heera. In the Ardhanareeswara, Purusha is the male principle and passive force of the universe, while Prakriti is the active female force. We are inseparable; we will always embrace and fuse with each other. Do you agree?'

'It is an unforgettable "mu dikhai" gift, Arjun. I am now unveiling my ghunghat for you, my charming prince,' Heera whispered into his ear. The memento was very special to her.

Heera then gave him a silver cup, containing milk mixed with saffron, crushed almonds and spices. He sipped some milk, embraced her and gave her the remaining milk from the silver cup.

'Marriage is a union of souls in which the individual bodies remain separate entities but the souls merge into one. Before the souls merge, why don't we drink the milk together?' The charming prince was at his romantic best.

'Why only milk? Let our bodies also merge into one like the memento you gifted, charming prince,' Heera tightly embraced him.

The two souls and bodies united. Their energies were replenished by the milk and they forgot the tiring rituals of the whole day.

The couple forgot the whole world around them and enjoyed their union, unaware of what awaited them the next day.

⌀

8

The next morning, Heera woke up early. She was whisked away by her mother, had her bath and got ready to leave with her in-laws for their home.

Arjun got up a little late. His sisters and cousins started mocking him.

'Arjun bhaiyya, was it too much work last night? Is that why you woke up late? The bedroom is much more difficult than the battlefield. Is it not?'

'The bedsheet tells us a story.'

'Bhaiyya, you are a warrior, hope you proved it last night.'

'Tell us about your experience!'

The laughing cousins Sainthavi and Sambhavi added more fun to the discussions.

'You are both going to experience it soon—your wedding is just three days away, my dear cousins,' Arjun was equally naughty in mocking them back.

Many jokes were cracked by his sisters, and there was fun and joy all around.

Everyone assembled in the palace hall for the *bidai* or farewell. This is the last event of the vivah, when the bride leaves her parental home. A coconut was placed under the bride's doli and the moving doli broke the coconut before moving further away. Heera removed her veil before she sat in the doli. Arjun offered her sindoor and covered her head with red embroidered veils, thereby declaring to the world that she now belonged to him.

The couple took the blessings of all the elders present. Heera's parents could not control their tears at being separated from their daughter. The tears were a reflection of both joy and sorrow. They were happy that their daughter was starting her family, but were sad that she was leaving them. A daughter's parents learn the lesson of exercising attachment with detachment in the natural course of their lives, when a daughter leaves them after marriage. They are attached to her to help her dreams turn into reality. They are detached from her as she has to learn to live with her husband and in-laws and treat them as her own family.

Arjun and Heera were about to leave for their new home. Then, like a bolt of lightning, came a shocking message.

∽

9

Medini Rai received the message from one of his commanders. He carried the news that he had heard on the outskirts of the fort. The message was clear.

Medini Rai could concede Chanderi and leave it to Babur, who had surrounded the fort with his men; or he could surrender to Babur with all his men and accept the rule of Babur. He would be given the new territory of Shamsabad if he accepted this option; or he could refuse these terms and face the army of Babur.

The whole palace was shocked. Medini Rai, being a seasoned warrior, first calmed everyone down and asked them to return to their rooms. He then convened an emergency meeting with his council of ministers.

'Harsha, what is your assessment of the situation here?' Medini Rai first asked his senior minister.

'Your Majesty, there are only around two thousand soldiers who guard this fort. There are about a thousand civilians comprising members of the royal family and aristocrats. We came here for the vivah and are not sufficiently armed to face Babur and his army in the battlefield. We have been caught unawares; the spy network has planted some false news that we are equipped with an army of ten thousand men. But the enemy will know the reality soon, Your Majesty.'

'Yes, Harsha, that traitor Silhadi who revolted against Rana Sanga, has now brought Babur here. He knew the vivah plans. He knew that we were not fully prepared here for a war. Anyway, we need to look at what to do now instead of focusing on why it happened.'

'Yes, Your Majesty, we have limited options before us. Fighting them is out of the question as we will definitely lose.'

'But leaving the fort is similar to a rat running into a hole in the ground. We are Hindu Rajput warriors; such fear is not in our blood. Also, surrendering to Babur will make all the battles fought till today meaningless. And accepting Shamsabad and Babur's rule is committing a great injustice to my mentor, my maharaja, Rana Sanga. I will die for him but won't become a traitor like Silhadi, my ex-colleague. By joining the invader Babur with a garrison of our soldiers at a crucial time of the war, he made our maharaja face treachery. Going to war with these unarmed unprepared forces will be a catastrophe. I have a fourth option in mind, Harsha.'

'What is it, Your Majesty?'

'The fourth choice is to take our fate into our own hands. We should not let our womenfolk be captured by them. We know for sure that they will be converted to the invaders' religion; they will be used as objects of pleasure rather than as human beings. They may become slaves in the hands of the invaders. Therefore, I have in mind the twin actions: jauhar for women and saka for men. The women will jump into a pit of fire and the men have to meet Babur's forces with full force and make them face our fierce battle. If some men do not want to go to war and be killed by the enemy, they can opt for mutual suicide, with our own men sinking their swords into their comrades. Let the saka be performed by men; either mutual suicide or attack, and let them face death.'

'Your Majesty, who will convince our people inside the fort?'

'I will assemble all the people at once.'

All the people quickly assembled in the open court. Raja Medini Rai addressed them:

'Fellow countrymen and women, we are under siege. The invader Babur has surrounded us when we have assembled here for the vivah.

We cannot win against them with the depleted strength of our army. We have been caught unawares. We should never let our caste and honour die. We should not let the invader take our lives. Instead, our women will walk into the fire of sacrifice without any fear. Let the jauhar stand testimony to our honour. Let the fire of sacrifice create flames of bravery in our men. Knowing clearly that their women will not be subjected to the tortures of our enemy, our men can attack the enemy camp without fear. The sacrifice of our women will unleash our men's bravery against the invaders. After the jauhar, we will apply the ashes from the bodies of our women on ourselves and unleash our strength.'

The crowd roared, 'Jai Mata Jogeswari! Long live Rana Sanga! Long live our Rajput rule!'

Medini Rai had delivered an inspiring speech. The palace was getting ready to make the great sacrifice. All of them instantly agreed to his proposal, since they were all keen to preserve their honour and dignity.

∽

10

Outside the fort, Babur's camp was restless. He received the message that Medini Rai was not willing to surrender. Babur was furious. He decided to wage a full-scale war and decimate Medini Rai and his men.

He called Ustad Ali, the head of the cannon and gun division.

'Ustad Ali, the water supply is coming from lower down the hill; you first cut the fort's water supply. Start deploying our artillery to break the fort walls.'

'Your Majesty, we are unable to find a position above the height of the walls. Hence, we have started building a mound to place the mortar on. The rest of the army has been asked to build ladders and mantles; we are getting ready.'

'That is good; assemble all our men. Let me address them shortly.'

Soon, Babur addressed his men: 'Comrades, this is a war against infidels. This is the mother of all battles we have fought so far. The Rajput forces will be decimated, and our conquest of northern Hindustan will take shape with this battle. After knowing the result of the war, all Rajput forces will accept our rule.

This place, which was a Dar al-Harb, a nation of non-Muslims for years, will now be made a Dar al-Islam, a Muslim nation. You raise your standards and win this war against the infidels. If you are martyred during this war, a place is waiting for you in heaven. If you are successful in this war, the heaven on earth, the fortunes of Chanderi, will await you. Get ready for an outright war!'

Saying this, Babur did something strange. He threw away all the wine bottles in his tent. He declared that he had stopped drinking wine from that day, in the name of the holy war or the Battle of Chanderi.

The atmosphere was charged. All the soldiers were wearing their emotions on their sleeves. Mustafa, one of the soldiers, asked his co-soldier, 'Those who are martyred in war will go to heaven. Do you know what awaits you there?'

'What?'

'Happiness, milk, honey, wine, gardens, flowers, rice, breeze... Young, beautiful, well-endowed girls with an excellent scent around them, who are there to serve us.'

'We will get these things here itself, if we capture Chanderi!'

The soldiers discussed the happiness that awaited them after the war, irrespective of whether they died or lived.

The war preparation was on in full swing. There was a keen determination in the minds of Babur's troops to capture Chanderi Fort by the following morning. The whole night the soldiers climbed the tall walls of the fort, while cannons tried to break the wall from another side.

During the night, Babur's scout reported a great deal of activity in the fort. They observed large masses of wood being gathered and assembled and great fires blazing behind the main fort walls.

Was Medini Rai trying a new kind of fire attack? What was happening inside Chanderi Fort?

∽

PART II

Baptism by Fire

11

nside Chanderi Fort, on the night of 27 January 1528, the area just outside the palace was buzzing with activity. A huge fire pit had been created. It was surrounded by wood. The surrounding wooden walls were set ablaze.

Heera asked her pregnant mother, 'Maa, have all the women agreed to enter the fire and sacrifice their lives?'

'Yes, Heera, the idea was initially mooted by our queen. The invaders do not treat the women of the defeated kingdom properly. It is not in their blood. The beautiful women would be kept by the men occupying higher positions, the other women would be sent to serve the normal soldiers. The women become slaves. They have to perform domestic chores and satisfy their masters' sexual desires as and when called. How can we accept such behaviour? The men and women captured would be auctioned at various slave markets from Delhi to Kabul. Death is much better. Is it not? Our brave soldiers will stand near the entrance. As the soldiers of the enemy enter, our men will fiercely cut them into pieces. Ours is a small force, guarding each entrance. We may not win, but we will create an impact on the attackers. We can kill many enemy soldiers, as our soldiers by that time would have given their women to the fire. They would have nothing to lose. They will be fierce in their battle,' she continued.

The flames of the fire were reaching the sky. The God of destruction, Lord Shiva, was at the centre of the fire. The women were entering the fire with their children. The queen was the first to enter. She fell at the feet of the king Medini Rai, and looked deep into his eyes. Their eyes spoke volumes. Medini Rai bid adieu to his queen. 'You go to heaven. We will come to you after fighting the invaders. Please keep the food ready and receive us in heaven. Hara Hara Maha Deva.' Then, the queen walked away from him into the fire.

The Vedic chants of Brahmin pandits filled the air. The male folk shouted, 'Hara Hara Maha Deva!'

The women and children were entering the fire pit, following their queen. The cries of 'Hara Hara Maha Deva' were reaching the sky. Would the lord of destruction listen to them?

12

While the other women were entering the fire wearing their wedding dresses, the newlywed Heera, her pregnant mother Meera, Sainthavi and Sambhavi were hesitant.

They took a step towards the fire pit and felt the flames on their faces. They paused for a second. For some strange reason, they all moved back. The other women behind them were embracing the flames of the fire.

Many thoughts crossed their minds. Meera thought that she had conceived after sixteen years. How could she kill her unborn child? How could she stop a child from living its full life? Heera thought about the previous day, when her husband had tied the mangalsutra in front of the sacred fire. How could she go from a sacred fire to a sacrificial fire in just a day? Her husband had gifted her the Ardhanareeswara statue, promising her that she would be a part of him. How could she go into the fire? She felt that all the prayers that they had recited on the wedding day would somehow save both of them. Sainthavi and Sambhavi had had their betrothal function just the a day earlier. Their gods would surely show them some way out of this.

All of them thought that they had to live their full lives, based on the reasoning each one had.

Heera asked them, 'Why don't we think of the stories of the pain inflicted by these invaders as false? They may be wrong. Our ancestors, like Raja Prithviraj, treated the women of defeated kingdoms very nicely. Why can't the same happen again now?'

Sainthavi agreed with her. 'Yes, there are Hindus living happily, paying the jizya tax. We can be one of them. Our husbands may be alive after the war. I still believe we can live an honourable life by paying the jizya tax.'

The pregnant mother, Meera, concluded: 'Our gods will not let us down. I want my child to be born to live its full life. Heera will have a brother, who will come with the karmic destiny of saving Hindus. Who knows? My intuition tells me that. Hence, we are not wrong in stepping back from this sacrificial fire.'

All these women came away from the fire pit. Hundreds of other women also did not enter the fire pit, hoping that something good would happen and that they could preserve their honour at the hands of the winning invader. Life is better than death, they all concluded. They all went to the Kirti Narayana temple, where hundreds of women, some of them with their husbands, had assembled. These men had also had similar thoughts and had therefore refrained from participating in the saka for men.

When they entered the temple, they were in for a shock.

❧

13

The golden idol of Narayana, along with a few others made of emerald and gold, was missing. They had been uprooted, along with the stone idol of Vishnu from the sacred sanctorum.

The main deity had been installed a few hundred years ago by Raja Kirti Narayana. At the time of installation, valuable jewellery made of gold and precious stones had been placed underneath the main idols by the king. All had been taken away.

Hare Narayana!

Who had taken them away, even before the invader had entered the fort? Had one of the citizens taken them away?

'I thought our gods would save us. Now we see our gods themselves uprooted by our own men,' Meera said, concerned. 'Who did it?' she could not stop herself from asking.

Everyone raised their voices in chorus. 'Your husband, the head priest of this temple and the palace, Bhargav Ram. The safe custodian became a thief himself. Your husband is the thief, worse than our invader. The day that Brahmin married you, a girl from the Vaishya community, I knew he had lost his sacred Brahminical virtues. I expected such unholy acts from him. Only our raja, Medini Rai, who supports these inter-caste marriages in the name of the unity of Hindus, raised him to the position of the head priest of the palace. Even if we give a dog a good bath with scented perfumes and keep him in the house, he will still move into the filthy piles on the street. The traitor ran away with all the fortune,' Mohanambal, the so-called pious Brahmin neighbour of Meera, spit venom on her.

Meera felt distressed. 'My husband, is he a bad man? Why did he run away with this treasure? Did he go with the intention of protecting it? Being a pious man, he would have taken it to protect it and not to steal it. But why did he not tell me, despite being fully aware of the fact that I am bearing his child and am in an advanced stage of pregnancy? Did he think that the precious idol was more important than the wife carrying his child and struggling with an advanced pregnancy? Why did he do that?' she wondered to herself.

So many thoughts crossed her mind.

'Is my husband a good man or a bad man? All his co-priests are here, willing to defend the temple and waiting to fight the invaders. Why has he left alone? Why has he taken away all the valuable treasures? Why he did not tell me even a word?'

14

Bhargav Ram had used a secret underground tunnel beneath the sacred sanctorum to flee. His escape was the hot topic of discussion across the palace among the people who survived.

Meanwhile, many men were getting ready for the saka. They applied the ashes of their women on their foreheads, placed a tulsi leaf in their mouths and started the ritualistic suicide event.

As Hara Hara Maha Deva was chanted loudly, Medini Rai called his minister.

'Harsha, pierce me with your sword. I will do the same to you. I do not want to die at the hands of the enemy. Let me die at the hands of my own men. Pierce me! Do not wait any more; let me start this sacrifice! Let our sacrifice lay the foundation of a great Hindu Raj in future. Hara Hara Maha Deva!'

Harsha plunged his sword into Medini Rai , who reciprocated. Both died on the spot. More mutual suicides followed.

Only a few hundred men decided to stand at the entrance gates of the fort and unleash their wrath on the invaders. Those who wanted to escape had all taken shelter in the Kirti Narayana temple. They were all praying to Narayana. 'Om Namo Narayana!' they chanted loudly the whole night.

The few hundred remaining soldiers woke up early in the morning, bathed, put on saffron uniforms, placed a tulsi leaf in their mouths and smeared their foreheads with the ashes of their wives and children. Then these men rode off to battle against the enemy. They did not want to allow themselves to be taken alive. They waited near the fort's entrance.

In the morning, Babur summoned his scouts to assess the situation. The outer fort fell into their hands quickly. Only a few security guards were seen at the gates of the outer fort. Babur's forces entered Chanderi Fort with hardly any resistance.

As they entered, they saw the dead bodies of hundreds of soldiers of Medini Rai. They realized that all these men had committed mutual suicide by thrusting their weapons into each other. There were bodies of dead Chanderi troops everywhere.

Suddenly, at this moment, there appeared around five hundred men wielding swords, who met Babur's forces at full charge. They were so fierce that Babur's troops were taken aback. A fierce battle ensued. But eventually the army of Medini Rai was defeated.

Babur's forces ransacked Chanderi Fort. There was rampant arson and robbery all over. Babur took charge of the fort. All hell broke loose.

15

The following morning, Babur ordered the tower of enemy skulls to be built, the practice formulated by his ancestor Timur against his adversaries.

'We need to not only record our victory, but also terrorize the opponents. No one will try to challenge us; instead, they will surrender,' declared Babur.

Meanwhile, his soldiers entered the temples, destroyed the idols installed there and killed cows over the temple deities. They captured all the people who were hiding there. All of them were paraded to the open ground in front of the palace. It was reported to Babur that some idols had been uprooted and stolen from their places.

The uncontrolled Mughal soldiers toyed with the grace of womanhood using their disgusting hilts. Babur visited the open ground where all the prisoners were lined up. He sat on a stage with his general.

'Comrades, we have crushed the rebellious forces. Those who still oppose us will henceforth hesitate to fight us. Now, let us get our prisoners identified. We have to select one of Medini Rai's men to identify these people. Whom do we select for that?'

His minister came running with a message at that moment.

'Your Majesty, our enemy Rana Sanga who escaped from us in our last battle was poisoned by his own rebel commander last night and has died.'

'Wah! Allah! When it rains, it pours. Both Medini Rai and his mentor Rana Sanga have died. We have no other enemies to challenge us in Hindustan. Announce this loudly to this gathering!' Babur ordered.

Meanwhile, Ustad Ali, the cannon commander, pointed at Keshav Ram, the priest with a tuft of hair on his head.

'Your Majesty, we have to first destroy these Brahmins, so that we can convert all these Hindus to Islam. They are the ones who teach their religious scriptures, and offer pujas to idols.'

'Bring him here, Ustad Ali,' Babur thundered.

Keshav Ram was brought before Babur. Suddenly, two Mughal soldiers caught him, opened his mouth wide with a stick and spit into his mouth.

Keshav Ram had long hair and a tuft because he practised Vedic rituals of worship. He was tied up on a wooden plank with his hair, and the table on which he was standing was suddenly lit up. After insulting his tradition, the Mughal soldiers burnt his hair first.

Before his body was about to be burnt, Keshav Ram cried, 'Please leave me! I will identify all these people, I will convert to your religion and obey you. Do not harm me any more.'

Babur signalled with his hand to stop further harassment.

'That is good. First, all the Brahmins should be grouped and should follow the process of the Darul-E-Mujmeen, purification by Allah, peace be upon Him.'

Keshav Ram was converted first and he became Kadar Basha. He first identified all the Brahmins in the group. Next, he had to identify the others.

He saw the women of the royal families first. He could not control his thoughts. They had lived in palatial mansions, but now they could not even sit near the palaces. Ropes were tied around their necks, and their strings of pearls were broken. Their wealth and youthful beauty, which had given them so much pleasure, had become their enemies.

Heera, her mother Meera, Arjun, Sainthavi and Sambhavi were identified. They were the only ones from the royal family who were still alive. The gathering was then split into two separate groups of men and women.

Keshav Ram, aka Kadar Basha, identified the heads of Medini Rai, his minister Harsha, and of the bridegrooms who were to marry Medini Rai's daughters.

Babur was very happy with the proceedings.

He declared, 'The victory shall be known as "Fath Darul Harabll" and engraved as a chronogram. The fort will be handed over to Ahmad Shah, the grandson of the sultan of Malwa. He has to pay fifty lakhs as khalsa. I am appointing Mulla Apaq as Shiqader, with three thousand Turks and Hindustanis under him to support Ahmad Shah.'

While he was speaking, the spy unit head came in and told Babur that the precious idols had been uprooted and that the head priest, Bhargav Ram, had run away.

'Where has he run away? He cannot escape from us. He knew we were coming. He has stolen the precious stones. Bring his wife!' Babur ordered.

Meera was brought before Babur. He looked at her, a pregnant lady who could deliver any time.

He asked her, 'Where did your husband run away to? Did you see your stone idol Narayana lying amidst the dead bodies? When your so-called God is in our custody, where can your husband go? He is a cheat. He stole the precious jewels. Did he not inform you? Where is he?'

'I do not know,' Meera answered in a trembling voice.

16

' Oh no, you are lying. Your husband could know how to give you a child at an old age but he does not know how to protect a pregnant wife about to deliver? What sort of a husband is he? He should at least stay with you. Instead, he ran away. I appreciate Keshav Ram and the other priests. At least they stayed with their wives. Your husband is a cheat. He ran away,' Babur continued addressing Meera with harsh words.

She could not control her emotions. She started crying. She was thinking that her husband had let her down. He had not informed her before leaving. If not for anything else, he should have at least cared for her, considering that she was pregnant and was due to deliver at any time. Even her God had let her down. No one was coming to her rescue. She began cursing her destiny.

Meanwhile, Babur declared that Medini Rai's twin daughters Sainthavi and Sambhavi would be converted to Islam. They would be called Sabha and Sadia henceforth.

'I gift them to Kamran and Humayun, my sons at Kabul and Delhi. Heera, the girl standing next to them, will henceforth be called Jahara. She will be gifted to Ustad Ali, the cannon wing commander. The royal family's male member, Arjun, will be sent along with other men to the slave market of Delhi. The other group comprising women will also move in another caravan to the Delhi slave market. All the commanders present here can select whoever they want in the Delhi market, free of cost. The remaining ones will be auctioned in the slave market there.'

With these words, Babur left for Delhi for a brief respite before the next battle. Heera was going with Ustad Ali, Sainthavi and Sambhavi were going with Babur to join his sons and Meera joined the caravan going to the female slave market.

Arjun was with the caravan headed to the male slave market. All of them were separated forever.

∽

17

The caravans carrying the slave prisoners from Chanderi were loaded with people captured in the battle.

Mohanambal, who had abused Meera the other day, was also travelling as a co-slave with her.

'Sorry, Meera, I used harsh words that day. You should not be blamed for the mistakes of your husband. I saw your plight as a pregnant woman on the verge of delivering a baby. See, your husband has run away. Now you are also a slave. Not only you, but the child you are about to deliver will also be born as a slave. Let us see what happens to us in the slave market. We do not know who will buy us.'

'What is this slave market? What will they do to slaves?' the innocent Meera asked her.

'Meera, you are too innocent. I heard about the slavery laws— they are very hostile laws from our perspective. Here is what I know about these laws:

- The right of Muslims to purchase and own slaves is absolute and unconditional.
- A Muslim man has the right to have sex with a captive slave girl he owns or a slave girl owned by another Muslim with her master's consent, without having to marry her.

- A slave's children cannot have inheritance.
- The testimony of a slave is inadmissible in court.
- Slaves require the permission of the master to marry.

'Oh no, everything revolves around sex. Are we mere objects of pleasure?' Meera could not control her anger.

'I can understand your anger, Meera. The women and children are sold as slaves to military men in various places, from Delhi to Persia. Even a poor Muslim household can own numerous slaves. There are major trading markets at Kabul, Kandahar and Delhi. Our caravans are now carrying us as slave *barda* to sell us at greater profits.'

'Disgusting! It is a pity we have to undergo this. Our gods are watching this plight of ours. When do we get liberation from all this, I don't know!' Meera sobbed.

'Now listen to me. I will tell you about their harems. The kings and nobles keep several women in their harems. They build beautiful gardens and flowerbeds in these massive harems, where dances and musical performances take place. Slave girls have two tasks to perform: domestic service and the provision of sex as and when required. Sex slavery and concubinage are almost interchangeable.

'For the polygamous Muslim men of means, slave girls and maids are in as much demand as dancing girls or concubines. Whatever the channel of entry into harems may be, the slave girls kept there are invariably good-looking. Their physical shape determines their places in the harem and in the master's heart. Their princesses do not wear the same dress twice. Once they have worn a dress, they give it away to the sex slaves at harems. The slaves are also trained in music and dance to entertain their masters. They are given pleasant names such as Nargis, Gulab, Chameli and so on.'

'Tell me, how do they select and fix the price of these slaves?' Meera questioned innocently.

'Oh, you will see that process once you reach the Delhi slave market. Our faces, sex appeal and the presence of bad breath and odour in our armpits—they smell us—all these serve as the criteria for selection and pricing. We, the old people beyond forty, will go for low prices; they will mostly use us for domestic work.'

'How big is this harem?' Meera continued with her questions.

'The size of the harem is dictated by a number of factors, including marriage and war. A large number of women servants come as part of the dowry when the king marries the daughter of a local ruler. Our entourage comprises a large number of singers and dancers. Many prisoners of war enter as slaves-turned-concubines. The harem owner, the noble or ruler, can pick up any one from these women at any time, for himself or for his guest, and they have to fulfil his lustful wishes.

'These harems do have their rules and regulations, Meera. The chief officer of the harem is usually a eunuch. All the harem officers will be ladies or eunuchs. Ladies from respectable noble families can work as supervising officers. The chief officer is responsible for the safety of the king and the nobles inside the harem. Well-built Turkish and Kashmiri women are employed on guard duties. All these cadres have fixed salaries.

'The harem complex is enclosed within high walls. There are fountains, ponds, gardens and orchards for women, many of whom spend their whole lives inside these harems. There are complex underground systems and well-ventilated chambers and passages. There are even underground cells with gallows erected in them to execute offenders. There are training facilities for music and dance, healthcare facilities and entertainment halls inside the harems.'

'Where do these eunuchs come from? Why are they employed in harems?' Meera asked Mohanambal.

'All over the Islamic world, the conquered men are castrated. This is done so that these men can guard harems and provide intelligence on the inside affairs of harems, as they have no hopes of having families of their own. Many boys of defeated Hindu kingdoms, who are sold to Muslim governors or rulers, are also castrated. Eunuchs also serve as guards for teenage girls who enter harems, all having been first converted to Islam.

In many places, when Hindus cannot pay taxes, they castrate their young boys and sell them in the market to pay off their taxes.'

'Oh my God! Why are we still letting these invaders carry out these atrocities on us? We do not know what is in store for us in the slave market at Delhi,' Meera was totally shattered.

They soon reached the slave market, where the happenings turned out to be rather unexpected.

18

The Delhi slave market was in a chaotic state. Groups of women were assembled and being showcased for sale. Army men, traders and nobles were walking in, inspecting and bargaining.

'For this girl, I offer five thousand silver tanka. She is good,' a rich Muslim noble quoted his offer. He was offered two more slave girls on sale. He checked their teeth and inspected them, but ultimately rejected them on the ground that they smelled bad.

'Get me girls like the one I already bought. She is well-endowed and has good looks, and smells like jasmine. Don't burden me with the useless ones,' he told the trader offering the girls.

The rejected girls were sold to soldiers and other men from

ordinary walks of life. They bought these rejected women at lower prices.

Even Mohanambal was bought by a rich Kabul-based soldier for providing domestic help at his house in Kabul. She had to leave for Kabul.

But Meera remained unsold. No one was willing to buy her.

'What can we do with this pregnant lady who is about to deliver? Why do these ladies get pregnant at such an advanced age? Let her first deliver her baby. Then we can consider buying her,' people remarked.

Meera was devastated. Her pain was bothering her.

'I think my labour pain has started. I am telling my child to learn to dance in the rain and not to complain about the storm. But I may deliver soon. This is a public place, the slave market. What can I do? Hey Bhagavan, why do I have to face these problems? My husband ran away. I am homeless, where do I go? Oh, the pain is unbearable!' she started crying.

But no one had the time to look at her. At this hour, a Sufi ascetic, a spiritual man full of compassion, arrived. He always visited the slave market whenever the slaves were assembled there. He led an ascetic life, running his own Sufi centre. Wherever possible, he lent his assistance. He was an embodiment of kindness and compassion and his assistance extended to people of all religions and walks of life. The inner law of Sufism consists of rules about the repentance of sins, the purging of contemptible qualities and evil traits of character and the adornment of the self with virtues and a good character.

Ameer Chishti, the Sufi ascetic, immediately sprang into action. He asked Meera to stay calm, telling her that he was there to take care of her. He frantically searched for another lady. He requested the trader who had just bought Mohanambal as his slave to spare her for some time on humanitarian grounds.

He immediately took Meera to a covered area, and asked Mohanambal to attend to her. She helped Meera push the baby out.

The baby was out, but wasn't crying. She placed her hand near the baby's nose to check its breathing. As she was checking, the baby started crying. It was a baby boy. Meera could not control her joy.

Mohanambal asked Meera to lie down for some time. She washed the baby, wiped away his blood and covered him with a towel to keep him warm.

Meanwhile, Ameer Chishti brought a trained nurse from a neighbouring hospital, who assisted with cutting the umbilical cord and other sterilization procedures. Ameer Chishti thanked Mohanambal. He took Meera and her newborn son to his Sufi centre. He told the trader that he would buy her for three thousand silver tanka. The trader was elated to receive that sum since he had thought that he would not even get five hundred silver tanka for her. Thus, Meera was sold to Ameer Chishti.

19

The Sufi centre called Khanqah was a dormitory run by Ameer Chishti in the suburbs of Delhi. It was run using donations received from spiritual members of the public. Students at Khanqah would pray, study and read together.

The major function of a Khanqah was that of a community shelter in areas where people from weak economic backgrounds stayed. Keeping a 'visitors welcome' policy, a Khanqah offered spiritual guidance, psychological support and counselling that was free and open to all. Hungry and depressed people were fed by a free kitchen service and provided basic education. By creating egalitarian communities, Sufis successfully spread their teachings of love, spirituality and harmony.

Ameer Chishti was the head of this Sufi centre. He brought Meera and her newborn son here, gave them a room and assured her that their comfort would be taken care of. Meera was completely floored by the warmth and affection shown by him. She started hating her husband Bhargav Ram who had just run away leaving them in the lurch. 'An unknown Muslim saint is showing such warmth, while my husband just abandoned me, when he was most needed,' she thought.

The following days were eventful. Ameer Chishti called one of his past students, Abdul Gafoor, a senior Mughal commander stationed at Shamasabad, in Punjab. Abdul Gafoor rushed to Delhi at the request of Ameer Chishti.

The Sufi handed over Meera and her newborn son to Abdul Gafoor. He told him, 'Delhi is still reeling from the aftershocks of the Panipat war. Members of the oppressed class are still being treated harshly. I want Meera and her newborn son to be taken away from the hustle and bustle of Delhi.

'I had to find a respectable gentleman to hand them over to. You came to my mind. Please consider her your sister and take care of her. I rescued her from the slave market by paying off the trader who was selling her. Something within me told me to extend a helping hand to this lady, who has been deserted by her husband. Take care, Khuda Hafiz.'

With these words, he handed them over to Abdul Gafoor. With tears in her eyes, Meera bid adieu to Ameer Chishti. With tears, Ameer Chishti bid farewell to them. They all moved to Shamasabad, located on the banks of the River Jhelum.

∽

20

Abdul Gafoor celebrated the arrival of his son Asif, who had been born just a few days back. He had been born on the same day as Meera's son. 'Strange coincidence,' he thought. The naming ceremony and thanksgiving function were being celebrated in his house.

The prayers were on...

'I pray only to my God, Allah, master of the earth and the sky. I will not pray to any other God. My prayers, my life and my death are all dedicated to my God, Allah.'

After the prayers, two goats were sacrificed. Abdul Gafoor prayed: 'Allah, when Mohammed Ibrahim, peace be upon Him, offered his son as sacrifice, you accepted the goat in his place. In the same way, please accept my sacrifice of these goats. Please accept the bones, blood and muscles of these goats as my son. This is my humble prayer; please bless my son.'

With these prayers, his son was named 'Asif' and a grand feast followed for everyone assembled.

At the same time, in the backyard of Abdul Gafoor's house, a naming ceremony was being conducted by Meera according to Hindu rituals. The child was dressed in new clothes. Some Hindu families who lived nearby were invited. Since the Hindus had to keep a low profile, very few attended the function. It was a Hindu boy's naming ceremony, being conducted in an Islamic commander's house. Since Abdul Gafoor had taken the responsibility of being Meera's caretaker, he did not want to deny any of her wishes. She wanted to pursue her Hindu way of living, so he facilitated that. He ensured that she followed her own beliefs with no intervention from anyone in his family. He gave her separate accommodation within his house.

The baby boy had to be handed over to the paternal grandfather or father who sat near the priest during the ritual. But unfortunately, no male member of her family was present.

Meera did something that no one had expected. She tied a rakhi on Abdul Gafoor's wrist and called him bhaiyya. She said that after King Porus had been defeated, his wife had tied a rakhi on Alexander the Great and made him her rakhi brother. In the same way, she was making Abdul Gafoor her rakhi brother. He was moved. She requested him to whisper to the newborn his new name.

He whispered into Meera's son's ear, 'Aditya'. He then announced the name loudly to all those present. Then the priest chanted sacred hymns to invoke the gods to bless the child.

Meera was very happy. She had refrained from entering the sacrificial fire pit only for her child. She was happy for Aditya, her newborn son, and wanted to give him the best. But she also realized that her son would have to undergo a baptism by fire as he would have to cope with several difficulties and obstacles on his path ahead.

PART III

The New Master

21

Meera and her son Aditya had settled into a small section in the backyard of the house of Abdul Gafoor. She pursued her traditions without any intervention from him.

A few times, she was seen outside her home by the Islamic moral police who noticed her continuing her traditions. They came to Abdul Gafoor and questioned him.

'This lady staying in your house, you claim that she is your sister. But she wears vermillion on her forehead. This is a practice of Kafirs. Advise her to refrain from such practices.'

But Abdul Gafoor could evade these queries since he was a senior military commander. One day, when there was a feast in his house, the wife of one of Abdul's deputy commanders saw Meera not eating the food served to the guests. She had cooked her own vegetarian food. She asked Meera, 'You don't eat cow meat? Have you not given up the practice of the Kafirs?'

Meera did not reply. But Abdul Gafoor intervened, 'Do you eat pig meat? The same way, Meera does not eat cow meat. Don't bother her.'

At times, the pressure became too much to handle. But Abdul Gafoor never forced her to change her practices. He even went to the extent of paying the jizya tax on her behalf, which allowed her to pursue her Hindu practices without any interruptions.

All these gestures from Abdul Gafoor further cemented Meera's bond with her rakhi brother. Meera came to the conclusion that Abdul Gafoor might have been her blood brother in her last janam and that was why he was continuing to shower his brotherly affection on her in this janam as well. She felt that she had never received this much love and affection either from her biological family or her family after marriage.

During these years, Abdul Gafoor never asked her about her past. That was his most wonderful trait. He never bothered her with those questions. His brotherly love and affection were pure, absolute and unconditional.

One day, she was deeply disturbed. She was crying in her room. Hearing her cry, Abdul Gafoor knocked at her door.

'Behen, why are you crying? Is there a problem?'

Meera came outside and stood beneath the mango tree in the backyard.

'No, it is nothing...today is my birthday.'

'Then you should be happy; why are you crying? Are we not taking care of you well? Have we not met any of your needs?'

'No, bhaiyya, I just thought of my parents.'

'I never questioned you about your past. Since you had been rescued from the slave market by my teacher, I did not want to dig into the past. Every slave must be thinking about their glorious past. I knew that, which is why I did not ask you any questions about it. It is the universal practice that a winning kingdom takes liberties over the losing kingdom. It so happened that you were on the side of the losing kingdom this time. There have been fights even between Hindu kingdoms in the past.'

'Never mind. You are now my brother—I will not hesitate to share my past with you,' Meera started recounting her past.

22

' I was born to a family of grain traders in Rewari in the Mewat kingdom. During the period of the *Mahabharata* in ancient India, a king named Rewat had a daughter named Rewati. She was fondly called Rewa by her father. He created a city called Rewa Wadi, named after her. When she got married to Balarama, the elder brother of Lord Krishna, this town was gifted to her. I was born in this famous city.

'My father Rai Puran Das Chandra was a small grain merchant there. My brother Hemchandra, also called Hemu, joined my father's business and expanded it by supplying to the army of the Delhi Sultanate. He also developed a cannon foundry in Rewari. He supplied saltpetre, the ingredient for gunpowder, as well as gunpowder and cannons to the Delhi Sultanate. I was the darling child of the family, as everyone felt that our business flourished after my birth.'

'Oh, then what happened?'

'I was attracted to Bhargav Ram, the young priest in the local temple. He was a great singer and I was attracted to his singing abilities. He is from an orthodox Bhargav Brahmin family.'

'Interesting, Meera, you had a love life,' Abdul Gafoor remarked.

'But that turned out to be the problem. My husband's father Koshal Ram used to buy grains from my father. Later, when my brother Hemu took over, he started focusing only on big businesses like supplies to the army, and he was not keen on small clients anymore. Koshal Ram could not pay off his dues to my brother, as they were poor priests who did not have enough money. When my brother heard about my love, he was furious.

'We were a Vaishya family growing in stature, directly supplying many goods to the Delhi Sultanate. This Brahmin boy did not even have the money to pay off his grain bills. How could he be expected to give me a good life? Moreover, we did not perform inter-caste marriages in our family. My brother ordered me to stop talking to him. However, love is blind. You don't love someone because they are perfect, you love them no matter how they are. I could not forget him. Even his family was against it, as they felt that an inter-caste marriage would deprive him of his Brahmin priestly status.

'But we decided to walk away from our families and get married. We had a happy marriage and had a girl soon after. During the Battle of Chanderi, I don't know where my husband went. The people of Chanderi say that he ran away. My daughter was carried away by one of your generals. I moved here to stay with you, carrying my son. But I can never forgive my husband for leaving me alone at the time of my delivery. This is my story, bhaiyya. I have lost all my relatives, but I have gained two new ones: you and my son.'

'Don't worry, behen, my whole family is with you. My wife Sabeeta and my son Asif are both fond of you and your son Aditya. Cheer up! Let us celebrate your birthday. Happy days are ahead.'

Meera's eyes were full of tears—tears of joy brought on by the fact that the people around her cared for her.

23

Meanwhile, Aditya was growing up with Asif, and their friendship was blossoming. Meera did not fail to notice certain special powers possessed by her son.

He could find hidden pathways and concealed doors in brick walls. He could tap the walls of the old palace nearby and enable Abdul Gafoor to find treasures hidden by defeated kings inside these walls.

He could create small underground tunnels at great speed and could create tremors on floors. On the river Jhelum, he could sense the shallows and potholes in the water and guide his mother to cross safely.

He once placed his ear on the ground and told his mother that one hundred horsemen were coming from a distance of 200 feet. His mother realized that he was spot on when she counted the number of horsemen.

He could even create landslides at will. He once created a landslide to stop a horse, while his mother watched in awe.

He once saw groundwater well technicians struggling to find where the groundwater level was high. He placed his ear close to the ground and pinpointed a suitable location. The technicians were astonished at the remarkable intuition of this young boy of six years. He was also able to move the underground water from one place to another when these technicians wanted to dig at another place.

Meera was extremely pleased with the special skills of Aditya. She felt that he would do extremely well in his career in future. He was God's gift to her, she thought. She considered him a panacea for all the sufferings she had faced in her life.

Once he turned six, Meera requested Abdul Gafoor to get her son educated along with his son Asif. The education was offered in a madrassa by Mullahs. From the age of six to twelve, Persian, Turkish and Urdu were taught to students. Islamic history and culture had to be studied. From the age of twelve to eighteen, the students who wanted to go to the army would be trained in military schools on various aspects of fighting: horse and elephant riding, archery, cannons and guns, spears and so on. Once they graduated from military school, they would be ready to join the army. Those who did not want to join the army could study trade, Islamic religious affairs or Islamic justice, from the age of twelve.

Both Asif and Aditya were pushed towards a career in the army.

However, Meera wanted her son to be taught the tenets of Hinduism as well. But where could she get that in an Islamic environment?

Both the children started going to the nearby mosque where there was a madrassa. Khwaja Moinuddin, the Mullah of the mosque, was also the head teacher of that madrassa. The children of senior army commanders and nobles studied under him. He took charge of teaching Asif and Aditya.

24

There were nine students in that madrassa. These students were attached to each of the three teachers. Khwaja Moinuddin, the head teacher, was assigned the three boys, Aditya, Asif and another student called Atif.

All of them were of the same age, six years. Their syllabus had the following subjects structured into a four-year curriculum.

- Arabic/Urdu language: Vocabulary and grammar
- Belief (Aqidah): The study of Islamic beliefs
- Character (Akhlaq): How Muslims are supposed to behave (a sort of moral science)
- History (Tariq): In the lower classes, they dealt with

myths about Islamic prophets; later they learnt about the Crusades and Islamic history
- Practice (Fiqh): Islamic rituals and law
- Memorization (Hifdh): Memorize parts of the Quran in Arabic
- Recitation of the Quran (Tajweed)
- Interpretation (Tafsir) of the Quran
- Statement about the Prophet (Hadith)

Aditya also started Islamic studies as per the syllabus. The children bonded very well. Initially they were reluctant to accept Aditya, since his Hindu name alienated him from the rest. Asif, his karmic brother and soulmate, intervened and ensured cordiality amongst all the nine students.

One day, Khwaja Moinuddin was alone with Aditya. The teacher was floored when he came to know of his pupil's land-focused special abilities.

'A blessed boy you are,' said the teacher.

At this point, Aditya raised a shocking question.

'Master, why are so many idols covered with paste stored in the underground rooms here in this mosque?'

Khwaja Moinuddin was shocked. 'How did this boy know the secret that had not been detected by anyone till date? He must be a boy with magical powers,' he thought.

He evaded the question. He told Aditya that he knew nothing of that sort. However, he said that he would check with his colleagues and let him know the next day. He asked Aditya not to discuss the topic with anyone till then.

The next day, he told his other students to take a holiday on some pretext and called only Aditya to the madrassa.

'My dear boy, I checked with my master. He told me that you are a blessed boy who has the karmic destiny of liberating the Hindu kingdom. He asked me to tell you the secret here, but on one condition.'

'Yes, of course, Master,' Aditya replied.

'You should make a promise on your mother whom you love.'

'What promise, Master?'

'You should never reveal these secrets at any cost. If you reveal them, your mother will face death, as you have promised in her name.'

'Yes, I promise on my mother and my God Narayana that I will never reveal these secrets to anyone.'

'Good! You said "Narayana". Do you worship him?'

'Yes, my mother has been given the special privilege of worshipping Narayana in our home, by my uncle, commander Abdul Gafoor.'

'Oh! Very good. The job is now easy for me—you will be fortunate to have a new master, an avatar of Narayana.'

'Is that so?'

'Yes, Lord Parasuram will be your new master, to teach you the tenets of Hinduism. Your mother is crying inside that she could not get her son educated about Hinduism. Now you have the fortune of learning the tenets of Hinduism. I will be your master for the outside world. But he will be your master for your inner world. He will make you look inwards, while I will make you look outwards.'

'Master, I am confused.'

'Don't worry,' Khwaja Moinuddin continued, 'listen to this. My original name is Kashyapa. I was forcibly converted to Islam by the invaders. I was a priest in a temple. They changed my name to Khwaja Moinuddin. There are many such priests who were converted and they all learnt the history, culture and religion of the invaders and are serving as madrassa school teachers attached to the various mosques all over our Bharat. We are all sleeper cells who will come out in the open on the day Hindu Raj is promulgated by someone amongst us. Until then, we will be in this camouflaged identity. You are the one who is going to work very closely with a great warrior who will liberate Hindus. Do you understand now?'

'Yes, Master, I understand vaguely. I have more questions running through my mind. I want to see the new master of my inner world. Can I know more about him? Can I see him?' Aditya's excitement was palpable.

⟡

25

Khwaja Moinuddin showed him the idols of the deities that were covered with a paste made from herbs and oils. This paste was applied in several layers to prevent the idols from being visible to the naked eye and to prevent them from being damaged by natural elements. These covered deities were then hidden from external visibility by a quickly constructed brick wall. Even if the wall was broken by any chance, the idol would not be visible due to the sand and paste, hence, would not be damaged.

'Where does this underground tunnel lead?' Aditya's excitement grew further.

'Look at this drainage hole. It is not actually what it seems to be. If you crawl through it, you will reach a forest nearby. Many small, precious and sacred idols which were taken away from several temples are buried under the trees there. They have all come from different parts of Bharat and are safeguarded by your new inner engineering guru, Lord Parasuram.'

'What? Lord Parasuram? When my mother was explaining the Dasavatar to me, she told me that he was the sixth avatar of Vishnu.

It is hard to believe that he is in the forests nearby.'

'Aditya, Lord Parasuram is one of the seven Chiranjivis. He will live in all the Yugas until the end of Kali Yuga. He will be the coach of the avatar Kalki. Until then, he will be meditating in this world. He has now come out of meditation to rescue the Hindus from their plight.'

'Master, can you tell me more about Lord Parasuram? Before I meet him, I want to know more about him.'

'Fine, hear me out, Aditya, this is the story of Lord Parasuram. Before I start the story, you should know the basis of the Hindu time cycles. The duration of the material universe is limited. It is manifested in cycles. A Kalpa is a day in the life of the creator, Brahma, which consists of a thousand cycles of four Yugas called one Mahayuga. It comprises four Yugas: Satya, Treta, Dvapara and Kali Yuga. The duration of each of these is 17.28 lakh years, 12.96 lakh years, 8.64 lakh years and 4.32 lakh years respectively, totaling up to 43.20 lakh years.

'These four Yugas, rotating one thousand times, comprise one day of Brahma and the same number comprise one night. Brahma lives a hundred such years. Fifty years of Brahma are supposed to have passed. We are on the first day of the fifty-first year. We are now in the Shvetavaraha Kalpa of the fifty-first year of Brahma.

'It is said that one Kalpa equals a thousand Mahayugas or fourteen Manvantaras. And one Manvantara equals seventy-one Mahayugas. We are now in the seventh Manvantara, named Vivasvatha Manrata, and in the twenty-eighth Mahayuga. In this Maha Yuga, Satya, Treta and Dvapara have passed. In Kali, we have passed 4,500 years out of 4.32 lakh years.

The number of years in each of the four Yugas is in the ratio of 4:3:2:1. The virtue levels of people are also in the same ratio. The number of avatars of Vishnu will also be in the same ratio: four avatars in Satya Yuga (Matsya, Kurma, Vamana and Narasimha) three in Treta Yuga (Vamana, Parasurama and Rama), two in Dvapara Yuga (Balarama and Krishna) and one in Kali Yuga (Kalki).

'Now you can understand that against this mammoth time scale, we occupy a miniscule part. Lord Parasuram was born as an avatar in the Treta Yuga.'

'Oh, our time cycle calculations are very interesting, Master. Lord Parasuram is a Chiranjivi living through the Treta, Dvapara and Kali Yugas. Please tell me how he was born and what the mission of his avatar is,' Aditya's excitement increased manifold.

26

'The exact birthplace of Lord Parasuram is contested, although the history of his lineage took place in the Haihaya kingdom located in modern-day Maheshwar. He is the Kula Guru of the Bhargav Gotra to which your father belongs.

'In the ancient times, the Kshatriyas, who used to be the rulers, became arrogant because of their power. Instead of ruling justly, they used their strength to oppress their subjects, levying unjust taxes and shirking their duty to protect their people. Ordinary men began to pray to Lord Vishnu about the conduct of these kings on Earth. Lord Vishnu heard their prayers and took birth as the youngest son of Sage Jamadagni and his wife Renuka. The son was named Rama. He performed a great penance to Lord Shiva and obtained a divine axe as his weapon. This axe became an integral part of his body and hence he came to be called Parasu (axe) Ram.

'He grew up like a typical Brahmin boy, studying the Vedas and other religious scriptures to become an ascetic like his father.

However, destiny had other plans. His mother used to fetch water from the river every day in a pot made of riverside clay. The power of her chastity allowed this pot of unbaked clay to hold water.

'One day, while she was filling water, she saw a handsome Gandharva pass by in the sky on his flying chariot. Renuka was filled with a momentary desire for this Gandharva. It was only a momentary thought in her mind, but she was no longer considered pure. The clay pot she had made dissolved in water. She tried to rebuild it several times, but to no avail. Afraid of facing her husband, she stayed by the river bank, wondering what to do. The yogic husband could sense what had happened. He asked his eldest son to kill her, as she had sinned in her thoughts. The son refused to do this, as he could not kill his own mother, even if she had sinned. All the sons declined to follow his orders. But when Lord Parasuram heard his father's orders, he immediately obeyed. With a sword in his hand, he beheaded his mother and all his brothers. The wrath of his father was appeased by his act. He told his son, "Son, whoever obeys his father performs an act of merit. You have done it. I shall grant you any boon. Ask for it and it shall be yours."

'Lord Parasuram asked for his family back, on the grounds that their crime had not been severe enough to warrant such a harsh punishment. He requested his father to show mercy. His father granted him the boon. The family lived together happily for a long time.

'During this time, Lord Parasuram's father had with him a sacred cow called Kamadhenu. He used to feed his guests with the bounties obtained from this cow. But one day, the cow was confiscated by the king, Kartaveerya Arjuna. He took the cow away so that he could feed his army freely. When Lord Parasuram's father resisted, the king killed him. Lord Parasuram and his brothers were not at home when this happened. The king was very arrogant. He believed that Kshatriyas owned the planet and that everyone simply had to obey them.

'When Lord Parasuram learnt about this, he seethed with uncontrollable anger. He vowed to cleanse the Earth of the curse of Kshatriyas. He began his campaign of ridding the Earth of Kshatriyas. His mythical axe was the most feared weapon among Kshatriyas. He went around the Earth twenty-one times, killing all the Kshatriyas he found.

'He accomplished his mission of cleansing the Earth of the cruel Kshatriyas who ill-treated people of other Varnas. Their kingdoms were taken away and donated to sages. He carried on this activity until the highest-ranking Kshatriya, Lord Rama, another avatar of Lord Narayana, came to rule Ayodhya. At that point, he transferred the spark of divinity in him to the new avatar. Later, in the next Dvapara Yuga, he fought Bhishma for not honouring his word to marry Amba, the girl he had promised to marry. He gave his astras or missiles to Dronacharya and Karna. Finally, he renounced all his worldly riches and started meditating for the benefit of mankind in the Kali Yuga. Now he is back, to save the common people currently being harassed by invaders.'

'That is interesting, Master, but why did he choose me as his disciple? When do I come into the picture?' Aditya asked.

'You should ask him that when you meet him,' replied his master.

27

A few months passed, but Aditya was not given access to Lord Parasuram, even though he had been promised so by his master. He was curious to know why this was so. Khwaja Moinuddin said, 'There are eight more students in the class. I cannot take you out separately. That would ring warning bells for the authorities. I have requested permission from the authorities to give you additional coaching alone, as you are from a non-Islamic background. Any time from now, I may get permission. Hence, we may have to wait.

'Also please remember that Lord Parasuram is now operating as a priest in a Shiva temple inside the forest. He is known as Ramdas to the few devotees who very rarely visit him. You are not supposed to talk about him or our activities at any cost. The moment you start discussing this with any outsider, your access to Ramdas Parasuram would cease. You have to be careful. You should not discuss this even with your mother.'

'I assure you, Master, I will never discuss these revelations with anybody at any time at any cost. I do not want to lose the opportunity to serve for a great cause. But I need clarifications on many questions before I embark on my new karmic journey.'

'All your doubts will be cleared, don't worry.'

As they were discussing things, a messenger came and delivered a message. They had finally received approval for the exclusive classes for Aditya. When Asif and the other students were informed, they were unhappy since they could not be together for some classes. The bond between them was becoming stronger day by day.

The next day, the opportunity which Aditya had been eagerly waiting for finally came.

Khwaja Moinuddin showed him a drainage hole. 'You can go inside this and you will find your way,' his master directed him.

'Inside this drainage hole?' Aditya exclaimed.

'Yes, you will see a different world inside.'

Aditya went in. For a few yards, he crawled inside the drainage channel. It was clean inside, as someone had diverted the drainage through other channels. After a few yards, he could see a door in the wall of the channel. He could see it only because of his special skills. It was so closely attached to the wall that it was not visible to the normal naked eye.

Upon opening the door, he found an empty room with a floor covered with sand. Removing the sand at a specific corner led to a layer of bricks without any cementing material. Beneath the bricks were two granite slabs serving as doors that could be opened by lifting.

Opening these doors led him into complete darkness. It was an underground tunnel that led somewhere. Aditya went through the tunnel for more than an hour. At last, he could see an opening that led him above the ground. He realized that he had come to a thick forest located on the banks of the river Jhelum. The forest was green with all kinds of trees, plants, flowers and herbs. The rays of the sun were piercing through the leaves of trees. The sounds of birds were pleasing to the ear.

He sighted a small Shiva temple in the middle of the forest. He went in and saw a sage dressed in saffron attire. His eyes were razor sharp, radiating powerful rays. Aditya realized that he was Lord Parasuram.

'Welcome, my young boy. I was waiting for you to come here.'

Aditya was awestruck by his majestic voice and was at a loss for words.

⟋⟍

28

'Come back to this world, my boy. You have come to the right place at the right time. Take a seat beside me. I know you want to ask a lot of questions to me. Come on, start your questions, my dear Aditya.'

Aditya was perplexed.

'Is this sage capable of reading my mind?' he thought.

Anyway, he proceeded with his questions.

'Parasuram Guruji, I would first like to know why you want me as your disciple now.'

'Aditya, the winds of destiny blow when we least expect them to. Sometimes they surge with the fury of a hurricane, while at other times, they barely fan one's cheek. But the winds cannot be denied entry into our lives. Now, the winds of your destiny brought you to me. Whether I will turn you into a furious hurricane or a cool breeze, I do not know.'

'Guruji, I do not comprehend.'

'Do not worry, my boy, I am Lord Parasuram. I was mandated to appear only at the time of the birth of the Kalki avatar at the end of this Kali Yuga. I have been assigned the task of receiving him and teaching him. Until then, I have to meditate here in the Mahendra Hills. But I have come out of my meditation long before the destined time. This is because of the acute problems faced by the people of Bharat at the hands of the invaders. I once destroyed the Kshatriyas for their oppressive governance. I am now back to take on the invaders. Your father pulled me out of meditation.'

'My father? He ran away, leaving my mother when she was carrying me!'

'That is what everyone thinks. The clouds had surrounded him till now. He is from my Bhargav Gotra family and is an upright man. Whatever he did was in the interest of the nation. I do not want to reveal his whereabouts or his current activities, as he needs to be shrouded in a veil of secrecy. A day will come when you will all realize the true character of your father Bhargav Ram, the man from the Gotra for which I am the presiding Kula guru. All I can say now is this: he briefed me on the cruelties inflicted by the invaders on the people of this land. He further requested me to mentor you, his son, whom he could not even see at the time of birth. That is why I chose you as my disciple at this critical hour. You are born to have a great impact on the people of this land.'

'I prostrate myself in front of you, Guruji. I totally surrender myself to you. Please guide me and shape me. I have received conflicting guidance from different people. My mother is totally against my father who left her abruptly. My adopted uncle Abdul Gafoor tilts my preference towards his rulers and their philosophies. Honestly, I am going through an identity crisis, Guruji.'

'You show remarkable maturity, my dear young boy. Confusion is the path towards clarity. Do not worry; no storm lasts forever. All you have to do is listen to everyone and take your own call; do not reveal the secrets we share here. Ask your questions. I will remove the clutter in your mind. Come on, ask your questions, my dear boy.'

Aditya became calm on hearing these powerful words from his new Guruji. He developed an instant liking towards his Guruji. At this young age, his mind had been oscillating between converging with the invaders' ideologies and diverging from them and sticking to his core ideologies, passed on from generation to generation. He realized that he would listen to his Guruji's answers for the various questions that were bothering him.

∽

29

'Guruji, where did my father meet you? How did he locate you, considering that you were meditating in solitude? Has anyone else met you in the Kali Yuga?' Aditya went on.

'Yes, my son, I will answer your questions. Your father has read the Hindu scriptures well. He often recites this shloka from the *Srimad Bhagavatam*.

> Aste dyapi mahendradrau
> Nyasta—dandah prasanta—dhih
> Upagiyamana—caritah
> Siddha—gandarva—caranaih

'Guruji, I understand this shloka means that Lord Parasuram still lives as a meditating Brahmin in a mountainous region known as the Mahendra Hills, having given up all his weapons. He is worshipped, adored and offered prayers to, for his exalted character and activities, by such celestial beings as the Siddhas, Caranas and Gandharvas. Am I right?'

'Yes, your understanding is correct. Your father is fond of me and recites the above shloka daily. When Chanderi Fort was attacked, the first thing he wanted to do was protect the precious idols that were once worshiped by Prahaladh in the Satya Yuga. He had been performing pujas there every day since he entered Chanderi Fort. For him, those idols were more important than anything else in his life.

'He took away those idols and was wondering where to put them. He had read somewhere that Lord Chaitanya had visited me in Durvasana in Dakshin Bharat, now known as Tiruppulani. As I am his Bhargav Gotra guru, he believed that I would come to his rescue. He believed that I stayed on a hill known as Mahendra Saala near Tirunelveli in Dakshin Bharat. He also heard someone say that I lived in the Malabar region there. He also knew that ordinary people have had no access to me and that only spiritually qualified people could reach me.

'He knew that his inter-caste marriage may have alienated him from other Brahmins. But I do not differentiate between varnas and castes in the Kali Yuga. This Yuga has destructions coming from invaders. It is a battle between Hinduism and the invaders.

'He came and prayed to me to grant him access. How could I have refused to help a disciple from my Gotra, calling me for a cause? I gave access to him. He handed me the precious idols which have been passed on from generation to generation since the Satya Yuga. He asked me to protect the idols and also alerted me about the risks they were facing. He also pleaded with me to groom his child who was yet to be born.

'I have been following you since your birth; you are now with me. I will honour my word to my Bhargav Gotra disciple.'

'Thank you, Guruji. Now I am clear about why you gave me access. My next question is ...'

'Before you start asking further questions, tell me, who is your role model today?'

'Guruji, I currently consider Babur my role model. He came from nowhere, but he captured our land and started administering it well. He won victories wherever he waged war.'

'Aditya, you have been brainwashed. Babur lost his throne many times at Farghana and Samarkand, places close to his hometown. He once became a fugitive with a following of just two to three hundred people. He captured Kabul and Kandahar. Later, he regained Samarkand. But he lost the support of his subjects and was defeated at Samarkand. Having lost all hope of retrieving his throne at Samarkand, he tried his luck in a different region towards the east, Hindustan. He has also had his quota of failures.'

'But he ultimately won in Hindustan. Have there ever been great warriors in Hindustan before?' Aditya countered.

∽

30

'Aditya, Bharata is believed to be the founder of the famous Bharata dynasty. He was the son of Dushyant and Shakuntala, whose love marriage is a well-known folklore. He was a great ruler with excellent qualities and the land ruled by him came to be known as Bharatvarsha because *varsha* meant land or continent.

'There have been many well-known rulers since the mythological days of Satya Yuga. Lord Rama and Dharmaputra were great rulers in the Treta and Dvapara Yugas. In the Kali Yuga, we have had great rulers: Ajata Satru, Chandragupta Maurya, Ashoka, Samudra Gupta, Rajaraja Chola, Krishna Deva Raya and many more. We have never had any dearth of great rulers. You should know that.'

'But then, why could the current rulers not defeat the invaders? Do we not have brave warriors? Ghazni, Ghori, Khalji, Tughlaq, Lodi, Suri, Mughal: why did we lose whenever foreigners invaded?'

'There were several Hindu warriors who bravely fought these invaders. Raja Dahir was one of them. His tolerance and liberal-mindedness enabled various religions to co-exist in his Sindh kingdom. This God-fearing ruler refused to return the people sheltered by him to the Arab states, from where they had sought refuge in his kingdom. This forced him to face Mohammad Bin Quasim in a battle. Bin Quasim had the support of various local tribes of the Sindh kingdom, namely, Jats, Meds, Bhuttos, and so on. Raja Dahir could not get any support from the other Hindu kingdoms, while his own state's local tribes lent support to the enemy. But he never ran away; instead, he stayed and fought until his death. When he was killed, his head was cut off and sent to the Caliph. There was no unity amongst the Hindu kings.

'They fielded chariots and elephants against the invaders who used fast-moving cavalry. Their attacks were quick and agile. The Hindu kings did not have a standing army on the lines of what Kautilya had recommended in his Arthashastra. In contrast, the Muslim invaders maintained their armed hordes in a state of permanent mobilization. Despite that, the Hindu kings fought an obstinate battle in the face of overwhelming odds. In Peshawar, Raja Jayapala lost to Mahmud Ghazni. He was released in exchange of fifty elephants. After the loss, Jayapala thought himself unworthy and burnt himself on a funeral pyre. This was a demonstration of the sense of honour which no Muslim invader could ever match.

'Further, the Hindu kings did not take advantage of situations on various dharmic grounds. Jayapala's son was defeated by Mahmud, but the latter had to return to his kingdom to meet an attack from the west. Jayapala's son could have taken advantage against his adversary and attacked him from the east as well. But he was too magnanimous; he went to the aid of Mahmud with a sizable force. Thus, he lost the chance of crushing the enemy and soon paid a price for it.

'Further, there is usually a stark difference between Hindustani and invading generals. Ghori was defeated by Chauhan, but instead of finishing him then and there, Chauhan allowed him to return. A year later, Ghori attacked him again. This time, Chauhan became overconfident and he did not seek assistance from other Rajput kings. Ghori knew his weakness and attacked him early in the morning, whereas, being a Hindu king, Chauhan followed set procedures of starting a war after sunrise.

'A few centuries ago, the Varna system became hereditary and a few classes began to dominate. If you are internally divided through the caste system, how can you counter external threats? Unlike the invaders' armies, our armies rewarded one's caste and not one's merit: Kshatriyas were taken into the army, regardless of their skills. It also did not matter to the lower class as to who ruled them, as all the Hindu elites were exploiting them.

'That is why Hindu kings lost to invading Muslim rulers. But this is not the end, fortunes will reverse once we all unite.

'Aditya, you said that you consider the invading ruler to be your role model. Are you aware of the extent of destruction wrought by these invaders on our society? We will see that in the next class. We shall meet every fifteen days. We should not let anyone become suspicious of your frequent visits. Take care, we shall meet later.'

Aditya returned to the madrassa the same way he had gone. His mind was revolving around the scintillating discussion.

31

The next few sessions went on according to the Islamic syllabus. The fifteenth day arrived.

The prayer session started:

Asathoo Allah Ilaha Illallahoo Vahthahoo
Lassary, Kalahoova Asathu Ahma Magammathan Abdhuhoo

'I pray to Allah, peace be upon him, to make me your pure devotee, and I will not pray to anyone other than you. You are the only God.'

All the boys completed the prayers, after which Khwaja Moinuddin took Aditya for the special class, while the other students started attending their regular classes.

Aditya reached the temple inside the forest and started asking questions to Ramdas, Lord Parasuram in disguise, his new guru.

'Guruji, you mentioned the atrocities committed by invading Muslim kings. It is quite natural that a winning kingdom superimposes its policies on the losing kingdom. Is this not normal?'

'No one should claim to defeat another person, Aditya. Just like us, everyone is made of the particles of Paramatma. Even if a king wins, how can he enslave a defeated king? Bharatvarsha faced many wars even before the arrival of these invaders. No one tried to impose their religions on the defeated kings. There are defined standard procedures as to how to treat a defeated king.

Yasmin Dese Ya Acharo Vivaharas Kulasthithi Tha Thaiva
Paribalyosow Yatha Vasa Bagathah!

'A winning king has to maintain the same societal culture, dharma and ethos that prevailed in the kingdom before the defeat. This is what *Yajnavalkya Smriti*, our ancient Dharmashastra, stipulates. The same is echoed by the great poet Kalidasa in his literary works and Kautilya in his *Arthashastra*. This is our *parampara*.

'Do you know what the invading Muslim rulers did to our society?'

'I have only heard some things, Guruji, please explain this to me.'

'Various methods exist with regard to the atrocities committed by the invaders, depending upon whether the iconoclast was in a hurry on account of Hindu resistance or had the luxury of time after victory.

'If a place was taken by assault, which was mostly the case, because Hindus seldom surrendered, it was thoroughly ransacked, its surviving population slaughtered or enslaved and all its buildings pulled down. In the next phase, the conquerors raised edifices for which the labour of enslaved Hindus was used on a large scale in order to produce quick results.

'Cows, and many a time, Brahmins, were killed, their blood sprinkled on the sacred sites to render them unclean for Hindus for eternity. Many masjids were constructed on the site, and with the materials from the temples. Temple sites and materials were used to build tombs for the eminent commanders who had succumbed in the battle.

'The invaders operated with the motivation of converting the whole of Hindustan to Islam. They were convinced that breaking a temple or idols was a good act that would lead them to heaven.

'They destroyed several temples: Srirangam in the south, Jagannath in the east, Benaras in the north and Somnath in the west; many other temples all over Hindustan were subject to their attack. They would stuff temples with wood without leaving any gaps. They would then set fire to them. The fire would destroy the temple and the idols and sculptures in it. The broken idols would be shifted and placed as steps in various masjids.

'The Hindus suffered at the hands of the invaders. They became slaves across the entire region from Delhi to Persia. They were traded like commodities in slave markets. Hindu women were used as sex slaves in harems. The princesses were taken away by the invading rulers and nobles. There are many such instances. The two daughters of Raja Dahir were buried alive in a wall. Many Hindu women self-immolated to protect their honour. Women with long black hair were humiliated by having their heads shaved. Besides the trauma of being windowed in an invaded land, the women had to bear continuous humiliations. Their lives were reduced to dust. Women were driven out of their grand houses, and nooses were put around their necks, the most humiliating tactic used by the tyrants. A whole valley in north-western Bharat is called the Hindu Kush. Hindu Kush means 'Kill the Hindu', which is a reminder of the days when slaves from Bharat died in the harsh weather typical of Afghan mountains, when they were transported to Persia.

'The Hindus who survived did not have any rights; they were second-grade citizens subservient to Muslims. They had to pay many special taxes. Those who could not pay their taxes had to go to the extent of castrating their young male children and handing them over to the taxmen. They would be used as eunuchs in various harems or sold in the market for eunuchs.

'The Brahmins were targeted. The invaders formulated a new theory which stated that killing one Brahmin was equal to killing ten other caste Hindus. They thought that destroying Brahmins would destroy Hinduism. Bhajans were stopped, and bathing in the Ganges was prohibited.

'The Hindus could not own weapons or ride. They were admitted to menial jobs in the military. Those who did not want to live under tyranny wandered like nomads in their own country, leaving their own houses. All the Hindu educational institutions were destroyed in various places. In short, in their own country, the Hindus became second-grade citizens, facing the brutalities of the invaders.'

'But Guruji, there are also good Muslims like my adopted uncle and his teacher, the Sufi saint. We were rescued by them. They treat us very well. My mother says she feels very happy with them and that she is leading a life happier than the early part of her life with her own family members.'

'Perhaps you are lucky to be interacting with such good Islamic personalities. But tell your mother to be careful, as they do not hesitate to sacrifice even their kith and kin for the sake of their religion. We shall continue our session in the next class. Now you go home, Aditya.'

Aditya left Guruji, but the discussion remained in his mind.

32

Aditya's next session with his Guruji was a month later. He started off with his question.

'Guruji, have the Hindus not tried to protect their temples from destruction?'

'Several innovative ways were adopted by the Hindus to protect their temples and idols. They covered the idols with a paste made of herbs and oils. This paste was applied in several layers to prevent the idols from being visible to the naked eye and to prevent them from being damaged by natural elements. Subsequently, the entire deity was hidden from external visibility by quickly constructing a brick wall around it, effectively sealing off entry to the sanctum sanctorum from all sides. Even if the wall was broken, the idols would not be visible because of the sand and paste, and hence, would not be damaged.

'Once, during the invasion of the Srirangam temple in Dakshin Bharat by Malik Kafur, the inner sanctum of the temple was fiercely protected by the Vaishnavas, who managed to hold off the army for three days, by which time a wall was built in front of the main shrine to hide the stone deity. Stone idols were buried under trees in a nearby forest. Even then, one idol was taken away by the invading army.

'A group of devotees, disguised as an entertainment troupe, set out to Delhi to retrieve the idol. The troupe put up a splendid performance in Malik Kafur's court, which was hugely appreciated by the sultan. In return, he offered them anything within the confines of the palace. They requested permission to take back the idol, taken away by the army from their temple. The sultan agreed to the request without hesitation.'

'Remarkable, Guruji—the deep devotion from them is highly inspiring.'

'Wait, Aditya, there are more such happenings from different parts of Bharatvarsha. The deities of the Jagannath temple at Puri in eastern Bharat were hidden underground with a sign of Dian Bar. These words, written in the Odia language, served the purpose of a secret code to help retrieve the deities at a later date. The main deity of Lord Jagannath had to be hidden elsewhere several times. Attacks on this temple continue to this day.

'Each time the invaders attacked temple towns, idols were hidden in different neighbouring towns and villages. They were hidden in new places each time to prevent them from being discovered. Even musical instruments like the mridangam became places to hide the idols.

'Secret underground rooms were created to store the idols. Sometimes, devotees would temporarily replace the idols made of gold and precious stones with fake ones made of clay and non-precious metals. The original ones would be hidden in secret chambers in the houses of certain devotees. Below the neem tree under which we are sitting, I am guarding several such precious idols, including the ones handed over by your father.

'In addition to all these, the devotees take part in decentralized worship to lower the chances of their towns being attacked. Rather than have one big temple in a town, idols of deities are distributed among devotees who have satsanghs and small-scale pujas in their homes. As the invaders' armies target rich and famous temples, this practice makes the towns less appealing to them, thus protecting the idols.'

'These are extremely interesting innovations, Guruji. But I still cannot understand this. The Muslim army men give their blood for their God. But are our Hindu people not ready to shed theirs to protect their God?'

Aditya's questions continued.

⟊

33

'Aditya, there are many instances of Hindu devotees shedding their blood to save their deities. In Hinduism, we do not attribute our sacrifices to our religion. In this religion, renunciation is celebrated. The essence of the Bhagavad Gita is this:

What happened yesterday happened nicely.

What is happening today is also happening nicely.

What is going to happen tomorrow will also happen nicely.

What have you lost?

Why do you cry?

What have you brought with you that you lost?

What have you created that goes to waste?

What you have taken is taken from here.

What you give is also given here.

What is yours today will become someone else's possession tomorrow.

Another day it will become some other person's possession.

Then why do you cry?

'We are trained to look at things in a philosophical way. The invaders think of how much more they need to be happy. Our scriptures teach you how much less you need to make yourself happy.

'These fundamental differences exist between the two approaches. We refrain from glorifying martyrdom. In fact, our scriptures do not even appreciate writing our own history. History is only a name and a memory. You are just a happening. That is why you do not get these glorified tales of the martyrdom of our own people.

'Do not think that only army men give their lives to protect their kingdom. Even people from ordinary walks of life gave up their lives to protect their deities.

'I shall narrate to you the happenings during the invasion of the Srirangam temple in Dakshin Bharat by Malik Gafur. I have earlier narrated how the idols were hidden from the invaders' eyes. But you should know about the sacrifices made by ordinary citizens during that time.

'The whole town was in a state of deep sorrow. Malik Gafur's army stayed near the Srirangam temple to take away the precious treasures therein. The temple was under siege. Many died fighting that mighty army.

'The temple followed the Devadasi system. The Devadasis are people who dedicate their lives to the Lord. They sing, dance and pray for Lord Ranganatha who is believed to live in the idol there. Vellaiammal was one such Devadasi.

'She looked like an angel, she was the most beautiful woman on Earth. Her eyes were so clear that you could see the rivers, the oceans and the world through them. Black hair, radiant and shining, swishing with every word she spoke. No flower, no Goddess could match her beauty. She had the body of a dancer, lithe and beautiful. With every step she took, she looked like she was floating. But her lips only uttered 'Ranganatha, Ranganatha', the name of the presiding deity of Srirangam.

'Suddenly, she became the talk of the town. Vellaiammal consented to sleep with the chief commander leading the charge against the temple. The town was shocked. How could such an ardent devotee of Lord Ranganatha take such an extreme step?

'It was well past midnight. She expressed her desire to meet the chief commander in person. She dressed up very well and went out to meet the commander in pitch darkness. The streets were deserted. Many invading army men were drunk and fast asleep.

'She walked into the tent of the chief commander and he woke up.

"Who is that?"

"Namaste, commander!"

"Oh, you have come here? Had you told me, I would have come to your home. I would be happy to take you to my harem. You are so adorable. I am looking forward to conquer you as well."

"No, commander, this is Lord Ranganatha's place. Here you should not touch me. You come to my home. You will have pleasure beyond measure. But before that, I have an important message for you."

"What is that message? I am only waiting to know where those priceless treasures are."

"Yes, I know the place where they are all kept, commander. I can reveal that to you on one condition."

"What do you want?"

"Before you take those treasures, I want to see them at least once in my lifetime. We shall see them together first. Only after that should you tell the others."

"Oh, is that it? Only the two of us will go. Also, you take what you want out of that treasure. We will take the rest."

'The commander was very happy. He would access the treasures that everyone was clueless about.

"Commander, come secretly without giving clues about our

movements to your army men."

'She went near the tower on the eastern side. "It is over here, but we need to climb up the tower."

"Come on, let us climb."

"There may be bats and birds that may trouble us."

"Why do you worry about these small things? If you are afraid of them, embrace me tightly. You will be all right," the commander winked. Both reached the top of the tower.

"What a panoramic view, Vellaiammal! The town glitters when seen from here. By the way, where are those treasures? Are they located somewhere on top of this tower?"

"Commander, look over there!" she showed him the sanctum sanctorum down below.

"Then why did you bring me up here?"

'In a fraction of a second, she suddenly turned violent. She pushed the commander from the top of the tower. He went crashing down and died. People from the ground below looked up. Vellaiammal stood like the aggressive Mahakali on top of the tower. The soldiers ran up to catch her. She was least bothered by them. Having achieved what she had wanted to, she jumped to her death from the top. The people of the town realized the sacrifice made by her. The men of the town became braver and fought the invader's army.

'The tower from where she fell has been named Vellai Gopuram in her honour. She showed the way to future generations, that they should not just sit back but should act in an appropriate way to counter invaders. In my opinion, she is a great leader who has shown us the way.'

'Guruji, this is a great sacrifice from an ordinary citizen. Unbelievable!' Aditya was stunned.

'It is the extraordinary conviction of ordinary people that makes them great. Great leaders realize the ideal, while many of us idealize the real. Are you going to be a leader who realizes the ideal or just a follower who idealizes the real? Think about it, Aditya.' The words reverberated through the whole forest.

∽

34

'Aditya, the invading rulers could not understand how such an unbreakable spirit dominated the Hindu communities. They would either kill themselves or find new ways of protecting their idols. They could not find out how their activities were financed in the absence of Hindu kings. Temples would loan their jewels to merchants for a fee. This helped keep the temples' belongings safe, while helping them maintain a steady flow of income. Deities were taken around remote villages in processions, and villagers would provide offerings in the form of agricultural produce. Merchants also contributed to temples from time to time. During invasions, temples would overtly as well as covertly exchange goods and services with one another for fulfilling and deriving mutual benefits.

'Aditya, are you now convinced of the devotion Hindus have towards their gods?'

'Guruji, partly, yes. Right now, I am neither attracted to my Hindu roots nor averse to the new religion Islam imposed on us.'

'Why?'

'Guruji, my doubts have not yet been fully cleared. Guruji, we say God lives in the idol. When Prahalad, the son of Hiranyakashipu, called out for God, Narayana appeared from a pillar. However, when idols and temples are broken and destroyed by the enemies, why is he not protecting himself? If he cannot protect himself, how can he protect others? Instead, ordinary citizens are losing their lives to protect him. This is the argument that the Islamic invaders are using to convert Hindus to their religions. Please help me understand, Guruji!'

'Good question, Aditya. But this is a wrong notion about God. Simply because our rulers lost the war, we try to blame God. They claim only one God who is theirs. That adds ego, self-pride and a keenness to destroy other thoughts. Mankind has to first look inwards. The greatest wars are fought in the silent chambers of our soul. Mankind must first cleanse itself from inside. Our Dharma has engaged in several debates: Truth, Ahimsa, Dharma, happiness, fulfilment, meditation, environmental consciousness and so on. Unless a person follows these Dharmas and is cleansed from inside, he has no right to talk about God.

'As God is transcendental and cannot be seen by the common man, he needs to exist in a form that can be seen, felt and interacted with by his devotees. This is the reason Arjuna, despite being a great devotee of Lord Krishna, was not able to see the Lord until he was given divine vision. The most common form God takes for his devotees is that of an idol. The idol is therefore that form of God which can be perceived by people who do not have the capacity to view God in his true form. He is present in different forms in different places. For instance, in Puri, he is present as Lord Jagannath, in Mathura he is present as Adikesava, and so on. The devotees do not see any difference between an idol and the God it represents. An idol is successfully placed in a temple, only after conducting various rituals and prayers to God. If an idol is successfully placed in a temple, it is believed that God himself has consented to be housed there. Hence, a temple is not merely a place of worship, but is a house of God.

'Another important tenet of Hinduism is that God is omnipresent. There is an Advaita philosophy that says God resides in every soul and that we are all manifestations of God. You can destroy an idol, but not every soul. You see the unbreakable spirit of each and every individual. No forces can destroy the God who resides in every soul. It is not in the idol but in every soul that he resides.

'God is present in all the elements of nature: animals, birds, plants, rivers and so on. That is why Hindus worship various forms of nature, in addition to idols. When man harms nature, it does not react immediately. It endures the pain for a long time, before even beginning to react. This is the reason calamities like earthquakes occur only once in several decades, despite man causing unthinkable harm to nature every day. This is not because nature is not capable of defending itself, but because it possesses a great deal of patience and strength. In the same way, God has patience and a forgiving heart because he wants to give invaders a chance to realize their mistakes and repent.

'While the invaders use the absence of God's response to state that God does not exist in idols and is not capable of protecting his devotees, the truth is that although God loves his devotees, and is by their side, he does not always come to their aid directly. When a child is in trouble, the father does not come to its rescue immediately, not because he does not care, but because he wants the child to learn on its own. This is what will truly help the child grow and develop into a strong and independent individual. Similarly, God's lack of direct involvement during invasions stems from his desire to inculcate in his devotees the virtues of tolerance, strength, resilience and determination, and to teach them to stand on their own feet and to protect themselves and their religion. Had he sprung out of idols and attacked the invaders himself, the devotees would not have learnt to fight their own battles and become their own masters. They would have remained weak and expected God to come to their aid, whenever they faced any problem. That would have been detrimental to their own development and security. He acted as a ray of light, guiding his devotees in the right direction and giving them the courage and strength they needed to fight the invaders.

'Fighting to protect their beloved religion and temples also helped devotees better understand the value of their religion and made them even more pious. They learnt to stand up for what is right, without allowing themselves to be misguided by the wrong people.

'You mentioned Prahalad; understand this: God appeared in the form of Narasimha, not to prove his existence to Hiranyakashipu, but to protect his pious devotee. God does not dance to the tunes of those who doubt his existence and his power. There is no need for him to prove himself to anyone. Hence, he did not have to respond to invaders, as they were merely testing him.

'Our mythology gives us enough evidence of the battle between Asuras and Devas. There may be momentary wins for Asuras but ultimately, God saves the Devas. Even here, Dharma will ultimately win. Adharma will make you feel it is winning, but in the end, it is Dharma that will win. You should have no doubts about that.'

Aditya continued thinking about the passionate arguments put forth by his Guruji during this class. A strange thing happened a few days later.

35

One evening, when Aditya was coming out of the drainage channel, Asif saw him. He promptly reported the matter to his father, Abdul Gafoor. They were worried that the channel was not safe. It was an alarm bell for them.

A thorough check of the channel was done the next day. It was business as usual. The drain was flowing through that channel. Khwaja Moinuddin told everyone that Aditya had fallen into the channel accidentally and had come out. The issue was closed as the authorities did not see anything suspicious.

This made Khwaja Moinuddin more cautious. It was decided that Aditya would make less frequent trips to the forests. A few months passed by. One day, when all the commotion around the drainage channel had died out, he went into it to meet his Guruji.

'What happened? Where were you all these days?' Guruji asked. Aditya narrated what had happened.

'Now you have turned twelve years old. Your theory classes are going to be over. From the age of twelve to sixteen, you will go through military exercises. Let this be your last class with me. When you want to see me again, I will come to you. I will be visible only to you and not to others. That will ensure that there is no suspicion around your activities.'

'Yes, Guruji. Today will be the last class here. I will exhaust all the other questions that I have.'

'You are an incorrigible person. You will never give up questioning, Aditya. Go ahead.'

'Guruji, there is a view that the Hindu religion does not follow the principle of equality. There are class conflicts and prejudices against women, unlike in the invaders' religion.'

'Who told you this? It is false propaganda that all the social illness is due to the principles of Hinduism. It is totally untrue.

'According to the Vedas, God is neither male nor female. God has no figure. Idols were created only to enable mankind to feel his presence. Most of us are not in a state to realize God, unless a figure has been given to us.

'There are as many female incarnations of God as there are male gods in the Hindu religion. Many Asuras, like Mahishasura for instance, were destroyed by female gods.

'Everyone says that Hindus have many gods. You have to understand that Hinduism accepts various *siddhantas* or philosophies. Even those who are atheists are accepted by it. There are various roads that lead to the destination of God. The roads may be different but the objective is one and the same. Also note that simply because Hindus are already exposed to many gods, they accept the worship of other gods as part of their philosophy. Many religions have been born in this Karma Bhoomi. Unless Hindus agree to the principle of coexistence, that would not have happened. You have to understand that. Although there may be tensions and wars between Shiva and Vishnu worshippers, do they ever ask outsiders to help them resolve their disputes? They all know that the different branches of Hinduism all come under one umbrella of Sanatana Dharma.

'You mentioned equality. The Varna system is not driven by birth. Valmiki and Vyasa, the authors of the *Ramayana* and the *Mahabharata*, are from lower caste families by birth. But they were recognized as great Maharishis. Land, knowledge and wealth was assigned to each of the Varnas, namely, Kshatriyas, Brahmins and Vaishyas. Those who are not covered under the three are called Shudras, meaning, the rest. The idea that one who controls land should not control the rest and vice versa was based on specialization of labour.

'But during the later years, when the Varna became hereditary, the caste system emerged. Those classes which had an upper hand introduced caste codes, making the Varna system hereditary. In fact, I once punished all the Kshatriyas for dominating over society.

'What should be blamed are man-made rules and not the Hindu Dharma. Dharma is static, while caste codes are dynamic and emerge over a period. We should not blame Hindu Dharma in general. Now, it is time to set it right and reinforce the principle of equality in Hindu Dharma. All the castes must unite to defeat the invaders. Our internal complications have to be settled by us and not by the invaders.

'You should know that the Advaita philosophy expounded by Adishankara does not recognize differences based on caste, creed, religion and gender, since we are all manifestations of God. How can such a religion be considered unequal? Out of the ten avatars of Vishnu, only one avatar, that is mine, was from the Brahmin Varna. The rest are from other Varnas.

'You have to note that the invaders' religion has different class conflicts. Sultans, ameers, gulamis, all of them have a different status in their world. These class conflicts are based on economic status. Those who are converted from the Hindu religion by force have the lowest status in their rule. How do you say that it promotes equality? You have been brainwashed by certain sections of people. Your foster uncle might have done that. These are wrong notions based on false propaganda.

'You may feel that practices like sati are against women. You must remember that the widows Kaushalya in the *Ramayana* and Kunti in the *Mahabharata* were the ones who led their sons to victory. Sati is a practice that originated recently. To escape the ill treatment of invading Muslim armies, the wives of Hindu warriors turned to this practice of self-immolation. They wanted to die with honour. Whose fault was it to push them into practising sati?

'You should know that those invaders who claim equality can marry four wives and can divorce them at any time merely by saying "talaq", and remarry. Apart from this, they can have concubines outside marriage. Their harems are full of sex slaves. Is this a way to treat women with dignity and honour?'

Guruji's feelings were so deep that the words came out like missiles. Aditya remained silent.

∽

36

'Guruji, you are an avatar yourself. Why don't you face these invaders head on and destroy them like you destroyed Kshatriyas in the past?'

'Good question, Aditya. I once went around the Earth twenty-one times, killing all the Kshatriyas who used to dominate others. Determined to pass on my knowledge of warfare to priests who could keep the power of kings under control, I even went to crematoriums and resurrected dead priests. All of them became my students. Many rishis shunned me, as they felt that I was contaminated with the blood of my victims. After those events, my anger subsided. I had accomplished the mission that was the purpose of my life. I met the good Kshatriya, Lord Rama, incarnation of Vishnu, and passed on the spark of divinity within me to him. Later, I taught Bhishma, Dronacharya and Karna in the Dvapara Yuga.

'I threw my bloodstained axe into the sea, but the sea recoiled in horror and drew back, revealing a new coast now known as the Konkan. All the avatars of Vishnu vanished from the Earth after their mission was accomplished. I am the only avatar destined to be a Chiranjivi, to live until the Kalki avatar arrives at the end of the Kali Yuga. Until then, I will be meditating for the benefit of mankind. I will be the Kalki avatar's coach. Until then, I am only supposed to witness events as they unfold. I have no capacity to take action on my own. I came out of meditation on hearing the prayers of your father. I am preparing you for the big task of setting up a Hindu Raj. I can only be a coach and not a performer.

'No one can display their powers all the time. Look at the plight Arjuna suffered after the war of the *Mahabharata*. After Lord Krishna's departure, Arjuna took the citizens of Dwarka to Dharma Raja's capital city Indraprastha. On the way, they were attacked by a group of bandits. Arjuna fought them, but he had already lost his divine energy and the power to wield his celestial bow Gandiva. Arjuna lost all his celestial weapons, and his inexhaustible quiver soon became empty because of the disappearance of divine energy following the death of Lord Krishna. Rishi Vyasa attributes this to the cycle of time. He says, "It is time that withdraws everything at its pleasure. One may be mighty, but becomes weak shortly thereafter. One may be a master ruling over others, but loses that position to become a servant who takes orders. These weapons, having achieved success, have returned to the place they came from."'

'Yes, Guruji, I wanted to ask this question. Where did the astras and mythical weapons go to? Can't they be used for countering the guns and cannons of invaders? Can I get that mythical axe of yours, Guruji?'

'All Divyastras are weapons of a single divine energy. This energy is chanted into the physical world by their wielders using certain mantras. When unleashed, they invoke all the raw power of a warrior's fury, infused with the Tejas of gods and are thus capable of laying to waste hundreds of opponents in one concentrated act of violence. Most divine weapons are named after the deities who preside over them with the particular powers that they reflect. But in Kali Yuga no one employs divine weapons. This is because of the potential amount of Tejas any given individual can acquire. The divine weapons have been withdrawn from circulation and returned to the divine powers.

'After the war of Kurukshetra, Vrishketu, who was the son of Karna, accompanied Arjuna. Arjuna treated him like his son and taught him about both the divine astras, Brahamastra and Divyastra. Vrishketu was the last person to know about the astras, because Lord Krishna told him not to pass on the knowledge of the divine weapons to the next generation, as the Kali Yuga was about to start and these weapons could lead to mass destruction later.'

'Guruji, does that mean I cannot get the mythical axe from you?'

'I will do you a special favour, since I am initiating you into the big task of setting up a Hindu Raj. Like I told you earlier, I threw my axe into the sea once my mission was accomplished. But the sea withdrew to form the land of Konkan. The axe must be hidden in the ground somewhere there.

'You can go there and search for it under the ground, using your special powers. You can see through the Earth and locate objects lying underground. But you can use that axe only for defence, to protect yourself and your things and not for killing opponents. That is the design of the axe for this Kali Yuga. I have undone its power to destroy, but its power to defend remains.'

'How can I go to the Malabar region now, Guruji?

'Do not go there now. During the next phase of training on military skills before graduation, Khwaja Moinuddin will undertake an educational tour to the Konkan region. You will find the axe there. You have my blessings.'

Aditya moved on to the next question.

'Guruji, will you not teach me military tactics?'

'Aditya, I will be with you till the mission of creating a Hindu Raj is accomplished. I went around the Earth twenty-one times to kill Kshatriyas. I will now be available one more time for you. But I will be with you for only twenty-two wars with the invaders. You have to complete the mission within that time frame. I stretched it to twenty-two wars this time, one more than those of my last expedition, as a special favour to you.

'During these twenty-two wars, I will always be with you, available at any time, anywhere, at your call. As part of military training, apart from enabling you to get my mythical axe, I will also teach you a special martial art. Using this, you can kill or disable your opponent by merely touching the correct 'marmam' or vital point. This art is called Kalaripayattu. This is mentioned in the *Rig Veda* and *Atharva Veda*. But very few knew of this art in the last Yuga. In the Kali Yuga, I am mandated to teach this to the Kalki avatar, as I will be his martial arts guru. But I am now deviating from the destined path and teaching you this in view of the pathetic situation currently faced by Hindus at the hands of the invaders. This will be my military training for you. I shall teach you, once you are done asking your never-ending questions, Aditya.'

'Guruji, I have come to the final question. Where do I go from here? What do I do? Will I be victorious in the new mission assigned to me?'

'Good, you have come to the end of my training session. You need to take the following steps now. First, you have to join your uncle Hemchandra or Hemu. Many think he is just an arms trader. But very soon, he will play a key role in setting up a Hindu Raj. Your mother may have pushed you to hate Hemchandra. He was once a caste fanatic. Now, having personally witnessed the plight of Hindus at the hands of the invaders, he has realized the need for uniting Hindus and shedding the caste phobia. You should somehow join him by convincing your mother. She may hesitate, but you have to prevail upon her. I will be with you for twenty-two wars, within which time you should accomplish the mission of setting up a Hindu Raj with Hemu. You should disclose neither your agenda nor your association with me. If you disclose either of these, you will lose me, my mythical axe and the special martial art taught by me. Next, you must listen to the *Ramayana* and the *Mahabharata* lectures by Bhagwan Das every week. He delivers lectures to a select audience at his home. I will tell him to add you to his list of attendees. You may face some turbulent, life-threatening events as you approach thirty. Therefore, you need to be careful when you reach that age. And, above all, be a lovable person, but don't become a slave; be sympathetic, but don't get cheated; be humble, but not a coward; be stubborn, but don't be angry; be cautious in spending, but don't be a miser; be brave, but don't be bad; be busy, but don't get perturbed; be dharmic, but don't become bankrupt; be wealth-conscious, but don't be greedy.

Finally, focus on your purpose, but don't worry about the outcome. God bless you, my son!'

With these parting words, the inward-looking training session from Guruji to Aditya came to an end. He also completed his formal training on Islamic studies successfully and moved into the final phase, the military training before his graduation.

PART IV

The Love That Conquers Hate

37

Aditya turned sixteen. The final phase of his education commenced. Several things were happening on the political front. The Sher Shah Suri dynasty took over control of Delhi and the Mughal king Humayun had to go into exile in Lahore and later to Persia.

Mughal control was now limited to parts of Punjab and they hoped that Humayun would recoup his forces and regain control of the Delhi Sultanate.

Aditya received military training in five main branches: infantry, cavalry, firearms, elephants and war boats. Aditya was given a first-hand experience of the various branches of the army along with his classmates.

The cannon was a very important weapon. It caused huge explosions that scared horses and elephants. This was helpful in disrupting an enemy attack. The Mughal army also depended on their cavalry for victory. Because of their speed and power, the cavalry was an important part of the Mughal forces. The rank and pay of officers was based on the number of horses they retained. The Mughal army was horse-oriented.

The boys were trained in horse-riding, elephant-riding and cannon operations. They were also trained to operate superior bows which could fire arrows over long distances, and they also received training about spy networks and ways to maintain the line of communication with the base, and so on.

The principal weapon of the armed soldier on horseback was the bow, particularly the short, reverse-curved bow that was common in Persia and Central Asia. These bows delivered substantial blows and had the highest penetrating power. The boys were well-trained in archery with the reverse-curved bow on horseback.

In addition to archery, the boys were trained in operating various other weapons: talwars, daggers, shields, gunpowder, cannons, muskets, mortars, maces, battle-axes and spears.

There were case studies and discussions about actual battles. Aditya turned out to be very strong in military formations, strategies and tactics. During a case study on the First Battle of Panipat, Aditya stood out among his batchmates. He articulated how the formations of Babur were superior to those of Ibrahim Lodi in that war.

This is how Aditya presented the case on the supremacy of Babur's military formation at Panipat. 'Babur reached the battle plain of Panipat first, selected the place of battle, and made the enemy come there. He stationed his troops in such a manner that the town of Panipat lay to their right. The houses and streets of Panipat provided a natural barrier against any possible surprise movement by the Afghan forces. Moreover, the town was useful to Babur in getting provisions and water for his men and animals.

'Babur fortified the left side by digging trenches and filling them with the branches of trees to give them the appearance of a regular ground.

'Seven hundred carts were purchased. Their wheels were tied together using ropes made of oxhide and they were placed in pairs in front of the army to give the impression of a virtual fort on wheels. This was an Ottoman technique which had been used by the Turkish sultan. The arrangement took the opponents by surprise as they had never seen such a spectacle before.

'Between every two pairs of carts, Babur set up six or seven mantles of wooden tripods, behind which stood matchlock men, ready to fire. Each of these was sufficiently large to protect one man, and gave special shelter to a musketeer or artillery man. The line of carts was not continuous. Large gaps were left at intervals to provide openings for a hundred to hundred and fifty men of his cavalry to charge through when required. The front was well defended by lines of carts and tripod stands and matchlocks. It was a point of strategy and a new system of defense which completely baffled the opponent and worked well for Babur.

'At the extreme ends of the line, spaces were left for his flanking cavalry parties to carry out charges against the enemy's rear guard.

'Babur's army was relatively small. Owing to this fresh strategy, excellent formation, superior bows which could fire arrows over long distances, excellent continuous communication with the base and the remarkably unified efforts of artillery and cavalry, Babur managed to defeat a large army of opponents.'

When Aditya completed his presentation on the uniqueness of the war strategy of Babur at Panipat, the whole class, including the teachers, gave him a standing ovation.

✍

38

While attending his military training classes, Aditya also went to Bhagwan Das's house to listen to his lectures on the *Ramayana*. He was allowed into the limited gathering on the request of Guru Ramdas.

Every evening, Bhagwan Das would narrate a chapter of the *Ramayana*. On one specific day, the session was on the entry of Rama and Lakshmana into Mithila with Maharishi Vishwamitra.

'As Rama and Lakshmana, the sixteen-year-old lads, walked

bravely and gallantly by the side of Sage Vishwamitra, all the women of Mithila dropped their work and ran to see the youngsters. It is said that the women who saw the shoulders of Rama saw nothing but his shoulders, while those who saw his forehead were mesmerized and saw the forehead alone, unable to take their eyes off it.

'It was at this moment that Sita and Ram looked at each other. It was a trance-like moment when their eyes met in a steady and unshakeable gaze. He looked into her eyes and she looked into his...'

While he was narrating this incident, his daughter Komal walked in with a cup of milk for her father, who had been lecturing over the last one hour. Her black hair was wavy and parted in the middle, her face was oval and her nose long and delicate. Her mouth was pretty, with rather full lips. She had a pink complexion reminiscent of a freshly blossoming flower. Her voice was lovely, a very unusual one. She was wearing a red sari. Her feet were not visible.

In the very same way that Lord Rama's and Sita's eyes met, Komal's eyes met Aditya's for a fraction of a second. But they felt like they had known each other for a very long time.

The shared gaze led to love at first sight.

Deep inside the eyes of a true lover lies the heart of a true lover, Aditya thought. The brain becomes illogical in the throes of a new romance. Love is blind for sure, he thought.

Komal had similar thoughts. He has the kind of face that stops me in my tracks, she thought. He is slim but muscular and a few fingers taller than me. He has distinct cheekbones and an angular jaw. His pale skin makes him look devilishly handsome. His curls are midnight black and his eyes dark brown, framed by graceful brows. Is he an emerging warrior? She went on thinking about him.

The two young lovebirds could not stop thinking about each other.

∽

39

The sessions continued. A few days later, when Aditya went to the house of Bhagwan Das, the lecture was on. Komal came to the hall and winked, hinting to Aditya to come out. She led the way. They reached the backyard garden, even as the lecture continued.

'You are so brave, you are calling a budding warrior to dance to your tunes.'

'So what? Warriors can show their power on the battlefield. Girls can show their power within the house,' Komal giggled.

'So, what is your name?'

'My name is Komal; what is yours?'

'I am Aditya.'

'Do you think you are Lord Rama? When my father was narrating how Rama met Sita, you were looking at me.'

'Yes, I was looking at my Sita. Is there a problem?'

'There is no problem. But like Lord Rama broke the bow to marry Sita, you have to break the phobia of my father.'

'What sort of phobia?'

'The Brahminical phobia. He is a fanatic of Brahminism. He will marry me only to a complete Brahmin. Are you that kind of a Brahmin?'

'Oh no, I was born to a Vedic Brahmin, whom I have not even seen in my life since birth. My mother is a Vaishya from a trader's family. Both my mother and I live in the house of Abdul Gafoor, the adopted Muslim brother of my mother. What do I call myself, a Brahmin, a Vaishya or a Muslim?'

'Oh, so complicated, Aditya. Then we surely have a battle to wage. You have to break a number of constraints before marrying me. Get ready for your first battle.'

'Komal, I am not concerned about what will happen. You are my wife.'

'Oh, do you love me so much?'

'Of course! Yes! I did not even bother to ask you about yourself. The moment I saw you, I made my decision. I feel as though we are continuing our relationship from our last janam.'

'Aditya, I also feel the same. Unmindful of the risks around, I have decided to marry you.'

Komal laid her face on his chest and Aditya warmly embraced her. Both of them forgot the world around them. Komal gave him a warm kiss, which was promptly reciprocated. As they heard the sounds of the people leaving at the end of the lecture, they came to their senses and parted.

The sparks of initial attraction were paving the way for the flames of deep love and affection between them. Would the lovebirds enter wedlock soon?

40

Aditya's hands were full. He started spending time with Komal in her backyard garden under the pretext of listening to the lectures of her father Bhagwan Das. His graduation was nearing.

One day, he heard from his foster uncle that his father had been sighted as an Islamic priest in a mosque in the Bundelkhand kingdom. He had converted to Islam on his own.

His mother said, 'What a man he is! He could have surrendered and accepted the conversion at Chanderi Fort itself. At least we would all have lived happily. But he ran away, and all of us got separated: him, your sister and us. Why would he do this? He never bothered about any of us.'

Hearing this, Aditya was disturbed. His Guruji had said that his father was a man committed to his religion. His Guruji was convincing him to participate in the struggle for the formation of a Hindu Raj. He was fanning the flames of a desire in Aditya to be part of the struggle for a Hindu Raj. He had come out of his meditation at the request of his father. But now, his father had made a fool of everyone.

'I am confused,' Aditya said to himself.

He felt like talking to his Guruji. His Guruji appeared in front of him as promised. He had assured him that he would be present whenever his disciple wanted him.

'What bothers you, my boy?'

'Guruji, I am confused. My father, your disciple, got himself converted to Islam.'

'Oh, you are confused about this? I still believe he is a man of conviction. Don't believe what you hear or what you see. Inquire deeply into everything. I can only tell you this much: he must have had some strong reasons for doing this.'

'Then why is it that I should support the setting up of a Hindu Raj, Guruji? As directed by you, I went on an educational tour with Khwaja Moinuddin and located your mythical axe in the Konkan region. I found it near Travancore, beneath the western range of the hills. What do I do now?'

'Aditya, I am here to remove your confusion. I have explained enough to you. I have no problems with any religion. But I am not for anyone superimposing their thoughts and forcibly converting others. Listen to this latest development.

'Humayun, your Mughal emperor, was driven away from Delhi by the Pathan king Sher Shah. Humayun decided that it would be wise to withdraw. He and his army rode across the Thar Desert when Hindu ruler Rao Maldeo Rathore allied with Sher Shah Suri against the Mughal empire. Humayun and his pregnant wife had to trace their way through the desert at the hottest time of the year. Their food stocks were very low. They had little to eat. He was heading to the Emir of Sindh, who had offered to help him. But enroute to the Emir's court, Humayun had to halt his journey because his pregnant wife was unable to travel further. Do you know who gave them shelter at that critical hour? It was the Hindu ruler of the oasis town of Amarkot who welcomed Humayun and his wife. It was in the Hindu noble's house that Humayun's wife gave birth to his son, Akbar. Humayun left his infant son in the custody of a Hindu Rajput foster family. You see the compassion of the Hindu ruler. He did not bother about the atrocities or the forcible conversions. For all you know, the Hindu ruler who once gave protection may now earn the wrath of the same people whom he had once protected.

'On the contrary, Humayun's brothers did not support him at this critical hour. This is the height of enmity among his own brothers, whereas a Hindu ruler extended his warmth in the hour of crisis on humanitarian grounds. Aren't you convinced that Hindus are to be protected from barbaric atrocities? I am asking you to support setting up of a Hindu Raj which will have to be a secular Raj, concerned with the welfare of everyone and the appeasement of none.

'Not only this, Humayun is now staying in Persia under the patronage of the Persian king. He is recouping his forces to bring Hindustan back under his control. In return for the Persian king's help, he has agreed to change into Shia Islam from his native Sunni Islam. Do you think that these people who change their convictions for personal benefits can be considered role models for you?

'Don't be confused by your father's conversion. It must have some strong reasons. For all you know, he might have been forcibly converted. Mainly to see you and his whole family, he might have succumbed to pressure. Until you know the real reason behind it after meeting him, you should not be confused. You should be unwavering in your commitment towards setting up a Hindu Raj. Do not oscillate in your mind. Be firm; you have great tasks ahead of you.'

With these words, Aditya's Guruji vanished.

∽

41

All nine boys from the madrassa graduated. After the prayers, degrees were awarded to them. Each of the nine students specialized in different fields.

Aditya specialized in military formation, strategy, intelligence gathering and tactics; Asif in cavalry; Atif in cannons and firearms; Aslam in infantry; Bashir in navy boats; Muhammad in elephants; Akbar Ali in spy networks; Sheikh Ahmad in weapon manufacturing and Basha Khan in Islamic studies.

His foster uncle and his mother both congratulated Aditya and Asif. They were proud parents. They knew that their children were about to pursue their careers after graduation.

But Aditya's happiness did not last long. A message came from Komal, saying that her father had come to know about their love for each other. He was extremely angry. His anger was further aggravated by the news of Aditya's father's conversion to Islam. He flatly refused the marriage proposal and kept Komal under house arrest. He was looking for an alliance from a Brahmin family and the boy was coming to their house the following week to finalize his marriage to Komal. Aditya realized that he could not delay any further. He sought the help of his foster uncle. Abdul Gafoor was completely in favour of his marriage to Komal. He convinced his rakhi sister Meera as well. He knew that he had to apply force. As a military commander, he used his power. He went to Bhagwan Das's house and told him point blank: 'You have to convert to Islam immediately. If you want to continue practicing Hinduism, then I can permit that with the continued payment of the jizya tax, but on one condition: you have to get your daughter married to my rakhi sister's son Aditya. She will walk out of your house and come with me right now.'

Bhagwan Das yielded to this pressure. Komal left her house and walked into Abdul Gafoor's house. The marriage was immediately solemnized the next day according to Hindu customs.

Meera happily received her daughter-in-law. Both Aditya and Komal were grateful to Abdul Gafoor and thanked him profusely.

They started a new life in a new house near Abdul Gafoor's house. Meera also moved in with them. She was seen shedding tears when she moved out of Abdul Gafoor's house, the place which had given her asylum.

42

Aditya and Komal started living together happily. They supported each other and enjoyed each other's company. Then the question of 'What next?' started bothering them. As a family, they had to become self-sufficient. Aditya had to take up a job. That was when Aditya considered working on his hidden agenda, as instructed by his Guruji. He wanted to float the idea of going to Delhi and joining the forces of Hemu, who had emerged as a leading gun and provision supplier to Sher Shah's army. He was slowly entering the corridors of power of the Delhi Sultanate. Hemu was emerging as the new star of the Afghan ruler, heading the intelligence wing of Sher Shah, in addition to being his key supplier of arms, ammunition and provisions for the military.

Aditya thought that his mother and foster uncle Abdul Gafoor would not agree. First, he floated the idea to Abdul Gafoor in a different way, concealing his real agenda.

'Uncle, I want to pursue a career on my own. I thought I could help the Mughal empire by getting them precise intelligence on Sher Shah. Since our Mughal emperor Humayun is recouping his forces in Persia to regain Hindustan, I can perform a small role to help him. It would be a tribute I could pay to you, my foster uncle. You gave me a home, education and all the love I could have ever asked for.

'Can I go and join Hemu, my uncle who rejected me? I can go with a camouflaged identity, win his goodwill and, at the same time, give you information of the developments in the Delhi Sultanate from time to time.'

'Brilliant idea; it did not occur to me. I fully endorse your views.'

'But please convince my mother, she does not want to see the brother who drove her away from home when she married a Vedic Brahmin.'

'Don't worry, I will do that. Have you discussed this with your better half?'

'I will, uncle. I'm confident of convincing her.'

'You can do one thing: when you go, adopt an Islamic identity, change your names from Aditya to Adnan and from Komal to Kamilah. I have a close friend, a senior Afghan commander in

Sher Shah's army. He is a commander loyal to the Mughals, planted by us as a mole in the Afghan Sultanate. He's Ibrahim Hassan, a good friend of mine.

'You can meet him and join his battalion first and later find a way to get close to Hemu, the chief of intelligence and procurements of the army.'

Abdul Gafoor immediately convinced Aditya's mother. 'He has a magical influence on my mother,' Aditya thought. Komal also agreed to his proposal. 'Everything is falling into place; these are good signs,' Aditya thought.

He also conveyed his plan to his Guruji, who appreciated the way he had got things done. His Guruji asked him to take the mythical axe with him and also assured him that he would immediately appear in front of Aditya whenever called.

Aditya and Komal, now called Adnan and Kamilah, started the journey from Punjab to Delhi. They carried Abdul Gafoor's letter to Ibrahim Hassan.

A new chapter in their lives commenced.

PART V

....

The Royal Connection

43

Hemu was born in a small town called Rewari in the Mewat region. His father Rai Puran Das Chandra was a grain merchant. Hemu was brought up to be a shopkeeper. The family was poor. He was brought up in a religious environment by his father. He had one brother and two sisters, one of whom was Meera, Aditya's mother.

Out of his personal interest, Hemu learnt Sanskrit, Hindi, Persian, Arabic and arithmetic apart from assisting his father in the grocery trade. During his youth, huge parts of Hindustan were under Afghan occupation. Vijaynagar, Rajputana, East Assam and Orissa were the only parts that remained free from the occupation of Afghans. In Delhi, the Lodi dynasty was ruling parts of Hindustan. Independent Sultanates ruled Gujarat and central Hindustan. The invaders inflicted many atrocities on Hindus.

Hemu started focusing on supplying Sher Shah's army. He started with food grains, then expanded to saltpetre, gunpowder and many other products. He wanted to attract the sultan's attention. His neighbours asked his father to stop his son from reaching the royal court. They warned him that Hemu was dreaming beyond his means.

But Hemu did not want to remain a grocer for life. Once he received the orders from the sultan's military, he developed a cannon foundry in Rewari and laid the foundation of a metalwork factory for brass and copper sheets.

This was the time when Hindus were forced to sell their grains to the state at arbitrary prices which hardly left them any profit.

Hindu merchants had to procure all sorts of merchandise from areas where there were no fixed prices. But the prices at which they had to sell to the state were fixed without any reference to the costs involved. Many a time, Hindu merchants had to keep their wives and children hostage at the capital to ensure that they brought regular supplies. The Hindu traders had to pay additional trade taxes, unlike Islamic traders who did not have to pay tax at all.

Hemu had to compete with such tax-favoured Islamic traders. One of his key competitors was Farooq Abdullah. This competitor tried to outsmart every supply offer Hemu made to the Sultanate. Farooq Abdullah was the president of the traders' association of the Mewat region. He replaced his cousin Syed Ibrahim, who had once given tough competition to Hemu. At a time when Syed Ibrahim was trying to drive Hemu away from business, he was suddenly killed by some unknown men. It was then business as usual for Hemu, even though some trade pressures came from Farooq Abdullah from time to time. Farooq Abdullah was a pan-Hindustan trader with excellent supplies and customer networks across various kingdoms, including those of the Mughals located in Punjab and Delhi when Humayun ruled.

In this hostile environment, Hemu had to outsmart many others. But Hemu not only survived in the market but went on to get close to Sultan Sher Shah. How?

44

Hemu once heard that the crown prince Islam Shah Suri, son of Sher Shah, was coming to Ferozepur with his reinforcements to crush the rebels. Ferozepur was not far from Rewari. On hearing the news, Hemu acquired all the grain from nearby areas.

The traders around him were wondering what he was doing. He was also refusing to sell grains to retail customers. They all complained to Hemu's father.

'Son, what are you doing? You are purchasing all the grains but not selling to retail customers. What are you doing? The whole bazaar's grains are in our godown.'

'Pitaji, wait and watch. You are doing this business on a small scale. I want to expand it and start a wholesale business. Wait and watch.'

One month later, as expected by Hemu, the crown prince Islam Shah Suri arrived with his army. He found that there was no grain to feed his army. He first approached the Islamic traders. No one had any grain in stock. The crown prince heard that Hemu had all the stock. The army would starve if supplies were not arranged quickly. The crown prince called Hemu.

'Do you have enough stock of grains to feed my army?'

'I have enough stock of grains, Your Majesty. Ever since I heard of the army entering our district, I have been saving grains.'

'Your foresight is commendable; what is your name?'

'Your Majesty, my name is Hemchandra; people call me Hemu.'

'Wonderful, Hemu, start your supplies.'

Hemu supplied to the crown prince without even raising the issue of price. Islam Shah Suri was pleased. He gave Hemu a handsome price upon completion of the delivery. Later, after crushing the rebels, the crown prince called him.

'I'm extremely pleased with your timely supply. You are a great planner. Why don't you come to Agra? My father Sher Shah would be pleased to be associated with an efficient person like you.'

'Thank you, Your Majesty! It would be a privilege to serve our sultan,' Hemu replied with great enthusiasm.

His father advised Hemu, 'Son, take care; life at court is full of intrigue. Don't trust anyone there. Be careful.'

'Why are you worried, Pitaji?'

'My son, a few years ago I lost one child, my daughter, who walked out of our house. It is still fresh in my memory. Meera was loved by all of us. When she left our house, I resolved that I will do everything in my power to prevent my children leaving me.'

'Pitaji, a few years have passed. Meera is still in our memory. On hindsight, I feel that I should not have been so harsh on her. What is so bad about inter-caste marriages, when our Hindu girls are being converted to another religion these days?'

'This is a welcome change, my son. You have mellowed down now. Will you accept her if you see her now?'

'Why should we talk about it now? Lots of things have happened. I understand that she is under the protection of an Islamic Mughal general in Punjab. I was against an inter-caste marriage. But she is in the care of a general who belongs to our invaders' religion. We have reached an irreconcilable phase, Pitaji. Let us leave that subject now.'

'All right, take care, come back successful. God bless you!'

'I will always be vigilant, don't worry, Pitaji.'

Hemu left for the royal court of Sultan Sher Shah at the invitation of the crown prince.

∽

45

'Your Majesty, I have invited this trader, Hemu, from Rewari. I wanted you to meet him, as he is a very resourceful man. In a short time, he arranged the supplies required for our army at Ferozepur.'

'Oh, very good. He seems to be an enterprising man. I drove Humayun away to Kabul. He may come back if rebels weaken the unity of my empire. For this I need the support of smart people like you.'

'Yes, Your Majesty, that will teach others not to oppose your rule,' Hemu replied with great respect.

'But, with famine reported from the northeast of Hindustan, we will have problems in the procurement of supplies for the army. Can you supply grains to the famine-struck regions?'

'Certainly, Your Majesty. Our loyal farmers would be honoured to supply to your troops. I will ensure that you receive uninterrupted supplies.'

'I will check your performance this time. If you do well, I will pass a decree to waive all the trade taxes applicable to you. Additionally, I will make you superintendent of bazaars of the Sultanate, do you understand?'

'It would be my honour, Your Majesty.'

Hemu immediately sprang into action. He undertook a whirlwind tour of Hindustan. He spoke to various farmers across kingdoms.

'Please set this grain aside for government troops. They will purchase in large quantities at fair prices. You need not sell to individual traders in the bazaar. The supplies are for our soldiers. Times are hard and food supply is of paramount importance now.

Would you be willing to supply? I will ensure that your supplies are exempt from trade taxes.'

Hemu spoke to various farmers across various kingdoms. All the farmers agreed to supply to him and he managed to deliver the quantity required by the army.

The sultan was very happy and exempted Hemu from the trade taxes. Sher Shah told his son, 'My son, Hemu is intelligent and resourceful. He can be a good asset for us, depending on how well we use him.'

'Yes, Your Majesty, I will see to it that we use him well.'

Hemu was consolidating his position. He became the exclusive supplier to the sultan's army. He supplied grains, weapons, saltpetre, gunpowder, cannons and other commodities. As superintendent of bazaars, he also brought about several radical changes in trade across the country, such as the introduction of standardised weights and quality yardsticks for products.

While he was consolidating his relationship with the royal family, a tragic incident occurred. During the siege of Kalinjar Fort of the Rajputs, Sher Shah ordered that the walls of the fort be blown up using gunpowder. However, Sher Shah himself was seriously injured in the explosions and passed away.

Upon his death, an emergency meeting of the nobles was convened and Sher Shah's son, Islam Shah Suri, was elected the next sultan of Delhi. Since Hemu had first been spotted by Islam Shah Suri, his position in the Sultanate was elevated.

46

Hemu's status in the Sultanate's affairs continued to rise. He was first made the surveyor of imperial kitchens, then superintendent of posts. Having excelled in these assignments, Hemu was looking for greater responsibilities.

Islam Shah Suri placed Hindus in command alongside Afghan officers, so that they could spy on each other, thereby ensuring that the controls were effective from the top. Recognizing Hemu's soldierly attributes, Islam Shah Suri made him responsible for army procurements and gave him a general's rank in the army. He was also given the specific task of monitoring the movements of Humayun's half-brother, Kamran, in the Punjab region.

At this stage, Aditya, alias Adnan, and Komal, alias Kamilah, reached Delhi with their secret message for the senior commander Ibrahim Hassan, the friend of Aditya's foster uncle, Abdul Gafoor.

'Welcome, Adnan and Kamilah. I have arranged for your accommodation near the Sufi centre run by Ameer Chishti, your uncle's teacher. You can meet me tomorrow at my camp and join my battalion. A few tests will be conducted by my assistants to assign you a grade. You must have had a long, tiring journey. Go and rest today.'

After thanking the commander, Aditya and Komal reached their accommodation. All the articles necessary for their stay were neatly arranged in the house. Adnan met Ameer Chishti and took his blessings.

No one knew their original names or the fact that they were Hindus posing as Muslims. The next day, Adnan went to the army camp. After a few tests, he was made a junior commander of cavalry.

A few months passed. Adnan's efficiency was praised by

various army commanders who interacted with him. Soon, he got an opportunity to showcase his talent in front of the royal army.

The army sports day provided Adnan a perfect platform. There was a live case study conducted at a sports event.

A big boulder was placed on the ground. On top of it, a small prototype fort was placed. On each side of this boulder were tanks filled with water. A soldier had to reach the fort and bring out a crown kept inside. The sides of the boulder were plastered with a highly poisonous substance. Anyone coming in contact with it would surely die.

This was a test for completing a successful siege. No one volunteered to even attempt. Adnan, being a specially gifted boy with the powers to deal with the Earth on his own terms, undertook the task.

He placed his hand on the ground in front of the boulder and shook the Earth. A mini earthquake shook the boulder and made the prototype fort collapse and fall outside the surrounding water tanks. The crown fell outside the tank. Adnan caught the falling crown and claimed victory.

The audience was stunned. He became an instant star. He caught the attention of all the family members of the Delhi Sultanate. Hemu, the chief of intelligence and army procurement, did not fail to notice him.

'Impressive, boy!' he exclaimed.

In spite of these developments, Adnan could not personally meet Hemu. He was waiting for an opportunity to meet him and join his team. The opportunity soon knocked at his door.

47

Sultan Islam Shah Suri called Hemu for a discussion.

'Hemu, Humayun's brother Kamran has established connections with the rebels in Ferozepur. There is a metal factory which makes weapons, swords, spears and axes for him. You go there and destroy the manufacturing base supplying him. There is speculation that Kamran plans to attack the town.'

'Yes, Your Majesty. I got this information from my sources as well. Let me go and finish them off.'

'Hemu, it should be a covert operation. You should not take a big battalion of soldiers with you. It will be a commando operation. That is why I am not calling the army into this. If an armed force is involved, there may be high collateral damage to the people living there.'

'Yes, I understand, Your Majesty.'

Hemu began building a team of young commandos. Suddenly, he remembered Adnan who had excelled in the military sports event. He approached Ibrahim Hassan and got Adnan on loan for a few days for the secret operation.

The team reached Ferozepur. The town wore a normal look. The people were not aware of the existence of the factory that supplied arms to Kamran or of his plans to attack the town shortly. Many guns and cannons had been hidden in the factory by Kamran for attacking the town. A huge cache of gunpowder was also being kept ready for him.

Kamran had planned to bring a small group of troops and attack the town at night, as in a terrorist operation and unlike a military operation. Since they had planned to come swiftly, they wanted to travel light and use the arms stored in the factory at

Ferozepur. If the supply from the factory was somehow cut off, they would be starved of arms and ammunitions.

Hemu knew that the operation had to be done covertly. He had a meeting with the young boys who went with him. Adnan suggested a plan.

'Let me suggest my plan. We must enter the factory as customers, since Hemu is the chief of military procurements. I will create a secret underground tunnel using my special powers. This underground tunnel will lead to the centre of the factory. Hemu and I will go inside alone, to avoid raising any doubts in the minds of the factory officials. All the other boys will be ready at the entrance of the tunnel. If need be, I will blow the siren at the factory gate which is blown every hour. The siren is usually sounded once for the first hour, twice for the second hour and so on. When I blow the siren, it will be a continuous sound with no interruptions.'

'Once such an alarm is sounded, the boys have to come inside the factory, fully armed. Hemu and I cannot take any arms inside, as we will be frisked at the factory gate. Hemu and I will assess the situation inside and deal with it accordingly.'

Hemu agreed with the plan. Hemu and Adnan went inside the factory as planned. As expected, they were frisked to check whether they were carrying any weapons. Both went inside as buyers of arms.

48

The factory was full of arms and ammunitions. They went around the factory. There were swords, spears, daggers and heaps of gunpowder everywhere. As they were looking around, they were suddenly surrounded by ten armed men. Neither Hemu nor Adnan had expected this. They were about to be killed.

'Are you the two devils sent by that Afghan ruler? Both of you are unarmed. You now get ready to go to hell. Are you the ones who were sent against our King Kamran? Wait for a day. The whole town will be destroyed. But first, you will start this march towards hell,' one of the men remarked.

'Wait, you all know we have no arms with us. You can kill us, but why don't you give us an opportunity to fight? If you have the guts, leave your arms and come fight us. We are two against ten of you. Why don't all ten of you fight against us without arms? I challenge that you will all be destroyed if you fight us without arms. Are you cowards? Come on, fight like men!' Adnan suddenly cried at the top of his voice.

'The two of you can fight the ten of us and win? What are you saying? We are not cowards. We shall lay our weapons down and fight you right now, come on,' one of the ten men shouted back.

What Hemu saw next was unbelievable. Adnan used the Varma Kalai or Kalaripayattu, a form of martial arts. According to this martial arts form, there are a hundred and eight pressure points in the human body, of which sixty-four are classified as lethal, if hit properly with fists. This martial art draws inspiration from the raw power and strength of five animals: the tiger, elephant, wild boar, snake and crocodile. Using this martial art, Adnan disabled and killed the opponents by merely touching the correct 'marmam' or vital point. The martial arts that he had learnt from his Guruji came to his rescue. With no weapon in hand, he had destroyed his opponents.

Hemu had vaguely heard about this martial art form, taught by a Hindu sage. But how did this Islamic man know it?

Hemu was confused. He decided to ask him the question after completing the task on hand. They had destroyed the men attacking them. What next?

Adnan was guiding Hemu like a seasoned crisis manager.

'We should destroy these arms and ammunitions. But we have security men guarding the front and back of this factory. When we destroy them, the gunpowder may explode and cause severe damage around the area. It has to be handled quietly. The people should not be aware of what is going on. It has to be a silent operation.'

'And what after that?' Hemu asked.

'We take the underground tunnel route and go outside. The opening of the underground tunnel I made is right here.'

Both of them came outside via the tunnel, where the team was waiting. After coming out, Adnan did not stop. He went around the factory, pressing his hand on the ground all around. He resembled a small child crawling with its hands on the ground. Suddenly, to everyone's surprise, the Earth shook for a while at the site where the factory was located. There was a fissure and the whole factory with all its men, weapons and gunpowder disappeared inside the ground. There were no traces of the factory.

'Excellent, extraordinary skill!' exclaimed Hemu.

'We have managed to complete the task without any hindrance to the public, as mandated by the ruler. Now, we wait for Kamran who will reach the factory soon, looking for weapons. We shall catch him alive,' Hemu declared.

∽

49

As expected, Kamran, Humayun's brother, came with a small force to capture Ferozepur the next night. He was arrested and brought to the royal court of Islam Shah Suri.

'Hemu, what can we do with him?'

'He seeks asylum in our kingdom, Your Majesty.'

'Asylum in my kingdom for Humayun's brother?'

'An enemy's foe is your friend, Your Majesty. He may be used to our advantage, Your Majesty.'

'To our advantage? How?'

'Your Majesty, Kamran is fleeing from his brother, Humayun. By helping Kamran, you can upset Humayun's plans of attacking us.'

'You are shrewd, Hemu. I will add the military strategy department to your portfolio.'

'Thank you, Your Majesty. I need some additional staff and I need your sanction.'

'I grant you the resources you want. You can take anyone from any division of our army. I issue an order to that effect.'

'I will do my duty to the best of my abilities.'

'Let Kamran stay as our guest in Punjab. If Humayun attacks us, make Kamran fight him first. But always keep an eye on his movements.'

'Sure, Your Majesty. I will make the arrangements.'

Hemu swiftly got into action. He ensured that Kamran was shifted as a state guest to the newly-constructed Rohtas Fort in Punjab. Rohtas Fort was one of the largest and most formidable forts built by the previous king Sher Shah Suri. It had large defensive walls and several monumental gateways. The fort was built atop a hill, overlooking a gorge where the Khan river met a seasonal stream called Parnal Khas. The fort occupied a strategic position between the mountainous region of Afghanistan and the plains of Punjab, and was intended to prevent the Mughal emperor from returning to Hindustan.

Hemu started building his team as directed by the ruler. He had three divisions under him: military strategy, intelligence and spy network, and army procurements. He selected Adnan to be a deputy superintendent of military strategy, his second sister Tara's son Ramaiya for the intelligence and spy network and Shadi Khan Kakkar for military procurements. Each of them, in turn, was allotted a few military trained staff.

Adnan gained a closer access to Hemu as he had desired. But he never revealed his real identity to anyone. No one knew about his Hindu origins. He was a practising Muslim for all those around him in Delhi.

Adnan and Kamilah happily lived as practising Muslims, completely hiding their real identity from the people of the neighbourhood. During this smooth phase of life, Adnan encountered an unpleasant situation.

50

One evening, Ibrahim Hassan, Adnan's foster uncle's friend, who had initiated him into the army of Islam Shah Suri, invited him to a music and dance performance. He went along with Ibrahim Hassan, leaving Kamilah at home.

They reached Chanderi Mahal, a closed complex with high walls. It consisted of a series of annexes designed in such a way that they were airy and comfortable, with a central courtyard for festivities. There were fountains, ponds, gardens and orchards inside the complex. All the apartments were interconnected. There was only one strictly-guarded entrance to the building. Most of the people inside were purdah-wearing women. There were eunuchs guarding the women and the complex. Adnan was unable to understand what this building was.

'Adnan, why are you wearing a confused look? You want to know what this building is?'

'Yes, of course.'

'This is a harem or zenana which was used by Emperor Humayun. His queen and important concubines have their own set of apartments here. They maintain their own household and compete amongst themselves to entertain the king. There are many other courtesans who live in dormitories.

'There are more complex underground systems of well-ventilated chambers and passages which open into apartments and are used to keep an eye on the harem. No male member is allowed beyond the concert hall. Only eunuchs run the safety, security and administration.

'Humayun married and brought the Princess of Chanderi, Sambhavi, here. Her twin sister was married off to his brother Kamran. They were converted to Islam after their father was killed. But once Humayun ran away, this harem fell into the hands of the new ruler Sher Shah Suri. But he gave it to my father, who was an ameer in his cabinet. My father passed it on to me after obtaining permission from the ruler.

'I come here occasionally to entertain my royal guests, nobles and army commanders. This was named Chanderi Mahal, since Chanderi princesses head these premises, with many conquered women from Chanderi working here as slaves.

'Today, we have a kathak performance in the concert hall.

That's why I brought you here. All work and no play makes life dull. You should also enjoy life, Adnan,' Ibrahim Hassan winked jokingly.

The kathak performance started. Something touched Adnan's heart. The Persian influence was visible in the intricate footwork, spectacular spins and exquisite expressions that are the major characteristics of this dance form.

The music and musical instruments that accompanied the dancers were influenced by Persian music and culture. It was a great performance from the artist. The song touched his heart. 'What a beautiful song,' Adnan thought. His mother used to sing it to him when he was young. It was a song composed by the saint Kabir.

> Ud jayega hans akela
> Jug darshan ka mel
> Jaise paat gire taruvar se
> Milna bahut duhela
> Naa jane kidhar girega
> Lageya pawan ka rela
> Jub howe umur puri
> Jab chutega hukum huzuri...

> The swan will fly all alone
> The spectacle of the world will be a mere fair
> As the leaf falls from the tree
> It is difficult to see
> Who knows where it will fall
> Once it is struck by a gust of wind
> When life is complete
> Then listening to orders, following
> Others will be over...

Adnan was perplexed. The voice was a replica of his mother's. Who was singing this song? The singer was behind the screen;

only the dancers were on stage. He could not control his curiosity. Who was singing?

~

51

A dnan's question was answered soon. The singer came to the stage and everyone applauded. Adnan could not believe his eyes. She looked like a younger version of his mother. Who is she? The question was running in his mind long after he had left the zenana. The next day, after finishing his office routines, he walked towards Chanderi Mahal. He knew that no men were allowed inside. But he could not waste any more time. He thought he would take a chance. He stood near the front door. The door was opened by a eunuch.

'What do you want? Men cannot come here. This is Chanderi Mahal, don't you know that?' the eunuch asked in a nonchalant voice.

'Yes, I know. But I am from Chanderi Fort. I think I saw my sister yesterday. She was singing a song by Kabir. The singer looked like a younger version of my mother and sounded like her too. I want to see her,' Adnan said in a husky voice.

'Are you from Chanderi?' the eunuch exclaimed, and opened the door.

'Yes!'

'I know who you are. You are the son of Meera. The person who sang yesterday was none other than your sister.'

'What? How do you know this?'

'I know this because I was once your sister's husband.'

'What?'

Adnan almost fainted. The eunuch secretly took him to the underground cowshed and asked him to wait there. Within the next few minutes, the singer, who was supposed to be his sister, arrived. The three of them were alone.

'Oh my brother! I could not see you at the time of your birth. I lost our father, then our mother. My life is ruined!' she started crying.

'Calm down, sister. How did you come here?'

'It's a long story. Once Chanderi Fort was captured, the twin princesses were converted to Islam and gifted to Humayun and Kamran, the two sons of Babur. I was gifted to Usman Ali, the cannon force head. My name was changed from Heera to Jahara and I was separated from my husband who I had just married. Usman Ali enjoyed me for one night. I was in early pregnancy at that time. I guessed that the pregnancy was from my cohabitation on the first night after my marriage to Arjun. Then, Usman Ali sold me to a courtesan from Agra. The courtesan saw my beautiful face and body and bought me, even though I was pregnant. I gave birth to a baby boy a few months later. They started training me over the years, working on my mind and my body in hundreds of different ways to please men. I was trained in Persian, Arabic and Urdu. I became skilled in composing poems, dance and music. I watched my mentor perform for the ameers. I was trained in make-up, dressing and a few methods to gauge the minute fluctuations of a man's moods. Not only that, I was also given lessons on seduction and forced to learn the art of giving enhanced pleasure to men through different postures.

'I was then forced to cater to a multitude of men. One day, an extremely handsome Mughal commander visited me and gave me the most joyous experience of my life. He spent many hours with me. He asked me about my early life. He came for a few days and gave me gifts. I became pregnant again.

'I had wanted to name my first son Vikram, a Hindu name, the shortened form of Vikramaditya, the great Hindu emperor. But I was told that I should give him an Islamic name, as he was born after my conversion. Hence, I named him Akram instead of Vikram. I named the second child Aamir, as he was born to an ameer, whose name I didn't know. That man suddenly stopped coming. I don't know if he was a Mughal warrior. I guessed so, since he left abruptly when Humayun was defeated by Sher Shah Suri.

'Then, my woes continued. Yet again, I had to serve new clients. Then, one day the man who had withheld his name from me suddenly reappeared. He said that Humayun would win again and that we would be together forever thereafter. He arranged for my placement in Chanderi Mahal, where I could act as his personal spy. I became a Kathak singer here. With the Chanderi princess at the helm, at least I am not forced to sleep with many men now. Occasionally, the unnamed warrior visits me and collects some information.

'My life goes on as a singer now. But I have taken a vow. I share secret information with our uncle Hemu because I want to see a secular Hindu Raj where all people have liberty. My sons should live in a glorious and free country.

'I have not met our uncle Hemu. I understand that he holds a senior position in the army of the current ruler of the Delhi Sultanate. My intuition tells me that one day he will form my dream Hindu Raj. Only with that intention do I operate as a secret information agent for his team. I exchange information that I gather from the various men, including the unnamed warrior companion, who visits me periodically. I pass on information through Arjun, my first husband, who is now a safe custodian of this property. He was emasculated and made impotent. It is quite strange that I give information to both competing groups. But I give the correct information to Hemu and the wrong information to the unnamed warrior, who wanted me to be a spy.

'But brother, please don't discuss my whereabouts with our mother. Let her at least assume that I live happily somewhere. Promise me that you will never discuss anything about me with our mother at any time.'

'How did Arjun land here?'

'That is another long story,' Arjun intervened.

෴

52

'I got married to Heera. We loved each other and dreamt of living together happily. On the first night together, I gifted Heera an Ardhanareeswara statue to symbolise that she will always be a part of me. But alas, the very next day we had to part with each other.

'I was sold as a slave to a Kabul-based trader at the Delhi slave market. He took me to Kabul and used me for some days to perform menial jobs. He forced me to convert to Islam and changed my name to Arafat. One day, he castrated me, emasculated me and sold me to an ameer's zenana in Delhi. When the ameer ran away along with Humayun, I was brought to Chanderi Mahal to safeguard its girls.

'One day, I suddenly saw my Heera among the girls I was guarding. We secretly met. She cried. I asked her which one of the children was ours. She told me her first son was our son. She narrated all the torture she had undergone.

'She asked me, "You promised me that we would be together forever when you gave me the beautiful statue. Why did you not

save me? We could have at least died together. Can we run away?"
That statue was safely kept in her room as a token of remembrance
of our first union.

'But I could not say anything to her. I was impotent; where
could I take her from this place? I told her that I would stay with
her as a security guard. That way, I could at least stay near her.
No one here knows about our past relationship. Our life goes on
like this with no end in sight.

'I take the information that she gathers from the various men
and give it to Hemu from time to time. Your sister did not want me
to reveal anything about her to Hemu, as she thought your uncle
may not even like to hear her name. Hemu has not recognized
me. I did not reveal anything about his niece, your sister. I just
listed myself as one of his voluntary spy network cells. Unlike the
women, I can go out any time.'

Adnan told them about his camouflaged identity as a Muslim
man serving the army. He received their assurance that they would
not discuss this with anyone. But he did not reveal why he was
using a camouflaged identity.

While the three were talking, the head security guard, an
African eunuch, saw them. He immediately alerted the security
team. They were arrested and kept in a separate underground cell
in Chanderi Mahal.

Adnan knew that they would be reported to Ibrahim Hassan,
the Mahal's owner. The guards did so and they were released in
a few hours. Normally, if a woman in a harem met an outsider,
she would face severe penalties. But thanks to Ibrahim Hassan's
intervention, no such thing happened.

'I told you to allot some time for play apart from your work.
I never thought you would implement it so soon. You should not
talk to any woman inside the harem. If you want anyone from
there, I can release her as your sex slave. Do you want someone?'

Ibrahim Hassan did not know that the woman Adnan had been talking to was his own sister.

'No, uncle, I tried to learn more about the song I heard a few nights back. I have a keen interest in classical music.'

'Anyway, do not get into such trouble again.'

'Yes, I assure you that I will not let you down for introducing me to your army, uncle.'

53

Meanwhile, Islam Shah Suri fell ill. Accompanied by Hemu, he went to his favourite resting place, Gwalior. Hemu took Adnan with him.

'Adnan, the sultan is on his deathbed and the prince is only a minor. The nobles have no unity amongst them. Humayun is just waiting for a chance to come back to Delhi. We have to be careful.'

Hemu's entire team was stationed in Gwalior. As the sultan's health was deteriorating, Hemu wanted his team to be alert in terms of intelligence and military strategies.

Hence, Adnan, Ramaiya and Shadi Khan Kakkar all shifted their base to Gwalior along with Hemu. They all stayed together in a complex forming part of the royal court.

One day, Ramaiya went to Adnan's room to call him for an urgent meeting. At that time, he saw a well-decorated Narayana statue there. He wondered what a Hindu God's statue was doing in a Muslim's house and felt that something was fishy. He decided to report the matter to Hemu and to carry out surveillance on Adnan. Moreover, he did not like that his uncle was developing a soft corner for Adnan. He reported the matter to Hemu.

'Uncle, I see you admitting Adnan into your close circles very quickly. You also discuss important secrets with him. We did not check his antecedents before recruiting him into our team. Who is he? Where has he come from? Is he trustworthy?'

'Ramaiya, you have to appreciate meritocracy. Adnan rose only because of his merit and the value he brings to the table. You got your position based on the fact that you are my nephew. You should not be jealous.'

'Uncle, I am not jealous. Today, I saw a well-decorated Narayana statue in Adnan's room. A practising Muslim does not worship such statues. I am doubtful about his origins.'

'Ramaiya, let me ask him. Don't jump to conclusions.'

Later, Hemu checked on this issue with Adnan. Adnan told him, 'We were converted to Islam from the Hindu religion only a generation ago. The statue was worshipped by my parents for generations. Just to give respect to our previous generations, I keep it with me. It is a token of respect for my grandfather. Simply because I converted, I cannot disrespect my grandfather who was a Hindu. Respect for the previous generation and practising Islam are two different things. Do you have a problem with this?'

Adnan asked a pointed question to Hemu. This set at rest the doubts raised by Ramaiya. However, jealousy did not permit Ramaiya to accept Adnan's fast growth. He carried out surveillance on Adnan. He was waiting for an opportunity to topple Adnan.

Meanwhile, Islam Shah Suri died at Gwalior Fort. Hemu felt the need to be careful, as any wrong move could ruin his career. The nobles assembled. The young infant prince was placed on the throne. He was murdered by Adil Shah, who declared himself the new sultan. Adil Shah thought differently from the previous sultan.

'I want to enjoy life. I cannot work madly all day. I should get an intelligent and hard-working person to take care of my government, while I continue to enjoy life. That man should not ditch me or overthrow me. Who can that be?'

At that moment, he saw Hemu walking into his royal office. Looking at him, a great idea struck Adil Shah.

'Oh! I have the answer. Here is Hemu. He is intelligent and hard-working. He will be a loyal subordinate. He also comes from a poor background, a humble grocer's family. He cannot topple me. Being a Hindu in the Sultanate, he is alone. He cannot get the support of my Islamic nobles and army commanders to topple an Islamic ruler. He is a safe candidate. I cannot trust anyone from my own religion, as they could get the support of nobles and topple me any time. I will make Hemu my prime minister. All will have to report to me through Hemu. Let him work, let me enjoy.'

He immediately announced: 'Hemu is appointed the prime minister of our Sultanate. All should report to me only through him.'

The sultan's decree created ripples in the royal court. The nobles raised their eyebrows.

'A Hindu prime minister in an Islamic Sultanate...disgusting! Our sultan has been brainwashed by the grocer Hemu. There will be a revolt across the Sultanate. Let us see how Hemu tackles these rebels.'

Very soon, an opportunity came for Hemu and his team to prove their soldierly qualities. Rebels across the Sultanate revolted against the sultan at many places, thinking that a weak sultan and a Hindu prime minister would not be accepted by the nobles and that the army would not take any stern action against them. The loud noises of war bugles were heard across the Sultanate.

Hemu the warrior had come into his own.

✑

PART VI

The Winning of Wars in Succession

54

After settling the issues at Gwalior and appointing Hemu as the prime minister, Adil Shah took Hemu to Chunar.

A messenger arrived with a message: 'Your Majesty, Junaid Khan of Ajmer, has rebelled against you.'

'He will be crushed!' thundered the sultan.

Hemu intervened, 'Your Majesty, I will take a small force with me. I will directly handle Junaid Khan.'

'Hemu, I appreciate your brave attitude. But you are not a soldier.'

'Your Majesty, my common sense and intelligence will lead to victory. Moreover, I want to lead from the front. Many army men here think that I am only a prime minister, I do not know how to fight. Respect is commanded, not demanded. Unless I prove my skills on the battlefield, I may not be respected by the army, Your Majesty.'

'Well said, Hemu! Go ahead, come back with victory,' the sultan encouraged Hemu.

Hemu and his team reached Ajmer.

Junaid Khan's council meeting was in progress. 'My lord, a grocer's son leads the sultan's forces.'

'What? The grocer's son has come? Tell that shopkeeper not to meddle with military matters. Let him focus on the weights and measures at his shop.' Junaid Khan laughed at the news of Hemu leading the military operations against him.

'My lord, please do not go out on the battlefield to fight this shopkeeper. I shall wipe out his army and capture him alive. It is not worthy of your stature to fight this trader,' his general, Daulat Khan, shouted at the top of his voice.

'Well said, my commander. You go and finish the job in a few hours,' Junaid Khan ordered.

Hemu was sitting with Adnan, Ramaiya and Kakkar in their camp.

'Do we pursue an offensive or a defensive strategy? What do you think?' Hemu asked his men.

'This is our first opportunity on the battlefield. We should prove our worth. Let us be on the offensive and destroy them quickly,' Ramaiya replied.

'I disagree here,' said Adnan. 'My view is that with a small force, we are not here to show our bravado. We are here to win. Since we have a small force against a large force, we should use more of tactics rather than direct attack. Tactics have to precede the direct attack, given our current situation.

'We need to emerge victorious because this is not just a battle against Junaid Khan, but against all those who question the credibility of our leader, Hemu. Hence, winning is more important than just showing our bravado,' Adnan was clear in his statement.

'Adnan, you are too young to know these matters. Don't intervene when experienced people like us are talking about strategy.'

Hemu intervened at this stage.

55

'Ramaiya, encourage the young minds. Adnan shows sparks of intelligence and he gives sharp strategic inputs. Do not demotivate him.

'Strategy without tactics is the slowest route to victory. Tactics without strategy is the noise before defeat. We need both. But an action without strategy and tactics is a disaster. A mere hope is not a strategy. The essence of strategy is what not to do.'

'Uncle, you always support Adnan, since he was right in the last few occasions. But he may not be right all the time,' Ramaiya chipped in.

'Ramaiya, the enemy should be struck at the weak spot. Currently, their weak spot is not in the numbers; they have them in plenty. The weak spot could be their complacency. We make them feel that we are too small to win. That will give them a kind of lethargy, a feeling that they have already won. We should hide our attention, as a tortoise withdraws his limbs and watches his enemy's posture. Let us be defensive and wait before attacking. What Adnan says is right. Take a defensive posture and create complacency in the minds of the enemy.'

'Adnan is always right for you, uncle,' Ramaiya's dejection was written all over his statement.

'I want to defeat the enemy; I do not want rivalries within our camp now. Let us hold a defensive position and wait.'

What Hemu expected did happen. Daulat Khan felt that victory was within his grasp. The taste of victory had gone to his head. At dawn, both opponents met. In the battle, Daulat Khan was slain.

'Victory to Sultan Adil Shah!' Hemu's army shouted.

When Junaid Khan learnt about the defeat of his men, he was

furious. 'Prepare to march with full force tomorrow morning!' he thundered.

Hemu consulted his team again. Adnan was the first one to come up with a strategy.

'We must win, our future depends on it. They have more men. They will also be more agile, shedding their complacency. We need to do one thing now, urgently.'

'What is that?'

'The enemy's camp must be planning for the war tomorrow morning. They will never expect us to attack them tonight. They must be thinking that we fought the war just this evening and even in their wildest dreams, they will not expect us to attack them tonight. The need of the hour is a surprise attack. Let us charge at them now, right now.' Adnan was firm in his conviction.

Hemu admired his strategic thinking. 'This boy is thinking beyond his age,' he thought. 'I agree. We cannot hope to fight the enemy by day. But if we make an effort tonight, we could rout Junaid Khan's forces. Hurry up.'

Hemu quickly selected a few of his strong men and slowly moved towards the enemy camp. Junaid Khan's team was fast asleep. The enemy was taken by complete surprise. Junaid Khan escaped by running away. Ajmer was captured by Hemu.

A triumphant Hemu returned to Adil Shah at Gwalior with his Afghan soldiers.

'Hemu, you have proven your mettle as a great warrior too. You are a man blessed with both courage and a sharp brain. All those who criticized you as a mere grocer have been proven wrong. Take these royal jewels. These are your reward,' Adil Shah proudly announced.

'No, Your Majesty, the reward should rightfully go to my fearless soldiers. Let them be richly rewarded,' Hemu replied. The sultan agreed.

All the Afghan soldiers who worked with him were very happy.

'Hemu leads from the front. He also gets us rewards, unlike other generals who take all the credit. We are happy to serve a leader like Hemu who rewards our work.'

The Afghan soldiers all talked highly of their leader, Hemu. But the nobles resented Hemu's growing influence. They were worried.

'This grocer seizes the Jagirs given by the sultan to us and redistributes them to ordinary soldiers. This is dangerous.' The Afghan nobles started complaining about Hemu.

While the nobles were resentful of Hemu's influence on the sultan, Ramaiya was resentful of the growing influence of Adnan on Hemu.

∽

56

Two nobles, Taji Khan and Fermuli, were having a heated discussion.

'We are not going to be favoured by Sultan Adil Shah anymore. That grocer is favoured by the sultan. He listens only to him.'

'I am leaving for Gwalior today to join the rebels,' Taji Khan told Fermuli.

'But I am going to stay here. We are still the sultan's favourite,' Fermuli stayed back.

Meanwhile, Kanauj district, under the management of Fermuli, was not being managed well. According to Hemu's advice, Sultan Adil Shah decided to shift Kanauj to Khan Sirpani. This enraged Fermuli. He went to the royal court with his sons and protested.

One of his sons stabbed the newly appointed Khan Sirpani,

who died on the spot. In the scuffle that followed, Fermuli and his sons were also killed.

Later, Hemu met the sultan.

'Your Majesty, Fermuli is a close friend of Taji Khan, who has left for Gwalior. He is sure to create trouble for us. We should stop him. He will join the rebels and try to declare independence in a few of our territories.'

'Hemu, we should crush him. Start immediately,' the sultan ordered.

Hemu led his forces and rushed to the Chhibrammau Fort, where Taji Khan was hiding. It was a beautiful rock building heavily guarded on all four sides by rebel Afghan soldiers, whose deadly arrows and sharp swords spared no intruders.

The planning team of Hemu sat in a tent, a makeshift arrangement, located outside the fort. Adnan requested Hemu's permission to take a few brave soldiers with him to sneak into the fort gates. How would he enter such a heavily guarded fort? Hemu's intuition told him to permit Adnan to proceed. He wanted to take that risk. He wanted to finish the operation faster, as he had to move to different parts of the Sultanate to crush the rebels.

Adnan requested Hemu to stay at least one mile away from the fort gates and enter only after he rang the fort bell. No one knew how Adnan would gain entry into the impregnable fort and win the forces inside, with only a handful of brave soldiers. But Hemu took the risk and permitted Adnan to move ahead. Ramaiya thought that this operation would destroy Adnan's life or at least his career. He felt that this operation would fail. As expected, Adnan had a tough time inside the fort.

57

On that new moon night, Adnan led a small yet fierce troop of young warriors on a quest to capture the fort. At this odd hour, the streets of the otherwise bustling city were blanketed in an aura of peace and tranquillity. The fort stood tall like an oak in the middle of grassland.

Adnan knew that it was next to impossible to enter through the fort gates, as they were all heavily guarded with hawk-eyed soldiers constantly keeping an eye on its surroundings from hidden balconies. Adnan's troops were vastly outnumbered by the soldiers in the fort, who also possessed sophisticated weapons. However, Adnan possessed something that could turn the tables in his favour: the element of surprise. At ten minutes past midnight, there would be a change of guard in the fort and this would be the time it would be most susceptible to an attack.

Using his special skills, Adnan created an underground tunnel quickly, leading to the darkest corner inside the fort. Using that tunnel, he and his troops were able to hide from the enemy soldiers.

Adnan went in and stayed inside the fort in a dark corner, waiting for the change of guard to commence. At the stroke of midnight, a new guard came to replace the existing one. As the guards were engaging in small talk, Adnan, along with a companion, stealthily approached from behind. Before they knew it, the guards found themselves landing face first on the ground, their consciousness quickly slipping away.

Adnan remembered his Guruji, who had taught him the Kalaripayattu, the classical martial arts. That art came in handy to knock out the guards on the spot without any noise.

Adnan and his men changed into the uniforms of the dead

guards and proceeded inside without any fear. They knew that they would not be easily discovered in those uniforms. Adnan's men then informed the other guards that they had seen a tunnel near the fort and suspected that the fort was under siege.

All the other guards, upon hearing this, rushed to different gates to check. Adnan, meanwhile, reached the watchtower that signalled any threats approaching the fort. Upon reaching it, he informed the head of the fort that some intruders posing as guards were spotted near the fort gates. Sure enough, the guards of the tower noticed people on all sides of the fort moving swiftly. From the height of the tower, they could not make out that the men near the gates were their own guards. They mistook them to be men from the enemy camp. Fearing that the fort was under attack, the head signalled to the archers to ready their bows. In the blink of an eye, swarms of razor-sharp arrows floated across the pitch-black sky before piercing the chests of the targeted intruders. Within seconds, nothing but corpses and broken arrows lay outside the fort.

The head of the fort flashed a haughty smile, proud of himself for having thwarted a potential threat. He even went around the room telling his subordinates how well he had managed to thwart the attempts of a siege by their enemies. In a few minutes, however, his pride and smirk vanished and his face turned white with fear. A guard had just informed him that the corpses near the gates were not those of intruders, but those of his own men. Before he had any time to react, he felt a strong blow to his head and collapsed. Most of the guards were dead.

Without wasting much time, Adnan rang the fort bell to alert Hemu waiting outside. The fort gates had already been opened by Adnan's men. Hemu entered the fort with his forces. Taking the palace guards by surprise, Hemu surrounded the fort. Taji Khan's forces surrendered, but he fled through a secret passage. He escaped to Khavasspur Tanda on the banks of the Ganges.

But this daring approach of defeating rebels in their own territory sent shivers down the spines of the dissenters of the Sultanate.

Hemu marched towards Khavasspur.

58

Khavasspur Tanda was located on the banks of the Ganges. Hemu, along with his sultan, arrived there.

'Your Majesty, Taji Khan has joined his brother's forces with about one hundred elephants. While running away from Chunar, he took possession of some of your treasures. He is now in Khavasspur Tanda with his brother.'

'We will teach them a lesson soon, Hemu.'

For a few days, the two armies waited on opposite sides of the Ganges without engagement. The Ganges was flooded. One day, a strange thing happened.

Adnan was thinking about his Guruji. He wanted to discuss with him what to do in the given situation. His Guruji had promised him earlier that he would visit him whenever he wanted. Adnan therefore appealed to him to appear before him. His Guruji appeared in front of him on his request.

'Aditya, oh no, Adnan now, isn't it? But I will continue to address you as Aditya. You have joined Hemu's forces. Have you got what you wanted?'

'Guruji, one correction: please say 'we' got what 'we' wanted. I joined Hemu on your advice. Fortunately, for whatever reason, my foster uncle Abdul Gafoor supported me on this. Hence, my mother did not stop me. It has been a while since last I met you, Guruji.'

'Do not worry. Now, you will see me far more often. You are on your journey towards creating a Hindu Raj.'

'No, it is Sultan Adil's Raj, Guruji. Hemu is too loyal to his ruler.'

'You will see the real Hemu shortly. By the way, why did you call me?'

'What do we do now? We are wasting our time, staring at the enemy. Both armies are merely marching along the banks of the Ganges. How long do we do this? Can we find some ways to attack?'

'You are a strategy expert. What is your strategy in this situation? Are you asking me?'

'Guruji, please do not make fun of me. You awakened me and enabled me to realize my special skills related to land. The martial arts you taught me enabled me to get closer to Hemu. My skills come from you. Without you, I am nothing.'

'Aditya, you are what you are. Your destiny is packed with duties. You are on your karmic journey. I was supposed to come out of my meditation only to receive the Kalki avatar at the end of the Kali Yuga. But your karmic journey brought me out of my meditation.

'Now, this is not the time for your strategy. It is the time for action, unmindful of the risks involved. This is a phase of action, not of thought. Hemu and you, along with your team, should use the elephants and cross the flooded Ganges. Your enemy is of the view that you cannot cross the flooded river now. They will be taken by surprise if you cross the Ganges and attack straightaway.'

'But the water is so deep, we may all lose our lives making this arduous journey. Should we take such a risk now?'

'Do one thing: you lead the journey across the Ganges, along with a small team comprising Hemu and his elephants. Take the mythical axe given by me. That will ensure you a safe journey. You will emerge victorious. This brave action will create waves of goodwill from all the soldiers, cutting across religious differences.'

While Adnan was talking to his Guruji, Ramaiya saw him from a distance. He could see him talking to someone, but no one was visible. As he always waited for opportunities to complain about Adnan, he promptly reported the matter to Hemu.

'Adnan, what happened? You seem to be talking to the air. Whom are you talking to? Has something gone wrong?' Hemu asked him.

'No, I was just praying. It is my normal prayer.'

'I heard you say Guruji. That is not an Islamic way of prayer. Are you concealing your identity for some strange reason? Who are you?' Ramaiya's pointed question came to him like an arrow.

Adnan addressed Hemu, 'These are wild accusations against me. Allah has ninety-nine names and whoever believes in their meanings and acts will accordingly enter paradise; Allah is 'witr'. The ninety-nine names of Allah, also known as the ninety-nine attributes of Allah, according to Islamic tradition, are the names of Allah revealed by the Creator in the Quran. I was praying by reciting these names. Maybe Ramaiya heard the words wrong. But why should he keep accusing me, spying on me all the time?'

'Ramaiya, you are accusing Adnan unnecessarily. Simply because you do not know his parents and his past, you keep saying we have not verified his antecedents. Hence you keep arguing that he should not be admitted into our inner circles. What is your problem? Listen to me. I see him being loyal to me; he brings great value to this team. I respect his privacy. Ramaiya, do not permit your jealousy to go too far. It will conquer you and destroy you. Henceforth, I do not want to listen to any other accusation against Adnan.

'All right, let us come to our situation. What is the best strategy now? How do we tackle our enemy stationed across the flooded river?'

'Please ask for one hundred elephants. We should assemble about a thousand soldiers, ten of whom are to sit on each of the hundred elephants. We cross the Ganges at night and attack the enemy. Permit me to lead the way on water,' Adnan requested Hemu.

Ramaiya and Kakkar had their reservations. But Hemu decided to pursue what Adnan recommended.

The sultan reluctantly agreed. This seemed to be a daring move. He even suggested Hemu to stay behind, leaving the task to his subordinates. But Hemu, who loved to lead from the front, decided to go. The team crossed the river. Adnan led the group with his mythical axe serving as a guide. To their surprise, the Earth beneath the water rose on its own and provided an elevated platform under the flooded water, which they could walk on. The flooded water never bothered them at all. They took the rebels by surprise. Taji Khan knew that Hemu was a brilliant strategist. He did not know that he was such a daring warrior as well, to have taken such a brave step. Hemu attacked the enemy camp in the middle of the night. The enemies were totally unprepared and were defeated. Taji Khan fled to Bengal.

'Well done, Hemu! Taji Khan will never dare to defy me!' the sultan thundered.

But the other rebels started creating a menace in different parts of the Sultanate. Meanwhile, Hemu declared that the elephant who had carried him would be adopted by him as his lifelong war companion. He affectionately named his personal elephant 'Hawai'.

The sounds of the war bugle, however, never stopped playing in Hemu's mind.

59

A new message was the topic of discussion at the sultan's royal court. Mohammad Shah, the governor of Bengal, had declared independence. The empire was beginning to fall apart. Adil Shah was very upset.

'Territory after territory is declaring independence. Sher Shah worked very hard to create this empire. It is crumbling now. I cannot allow this to happen.'

'Your Majesty, please stay at Chunar and watch the developments in Delhi. Please permit me to go to Bengal and tame Mohammad Shah. Please do not worry. I will give my blood to ensure that our empire is stable and flourishing for many years to come.'

Hemu left for Bengal with his forces. Yet another war began.

As Hemu was proceeding towards Bengal, Mohammad Shah came down towards Chhapparghatta near Kapi on the banks of the Yamuna. Adil Shah called Hemu back. Hemu took on the forces of Mohammad Shah.

The enemy fort was protected on all sides. The rear was bound by the flooded Yamuna and was relatively less protected. Hence, capturing the fort from the side of the Yamuna would be the most effective way, as conceived by Adnan. This was endorsed by Hemu as well.

But how could they cross the flooded river? It was not like the earlier operation, where a few men had to be transported on elephants. In this operation, the whole army had to be shifted across the river.

Adnan introspected and was reminded by his Guruji of his special skill to build underground tunnels in short spans of time. Adnan built an underground tunnel below the Yamuna and transported all the troops to the rear of the fort, while Mohammad Shah was with his troops on the three other sides, leaving the rear unguarded. He had felt that there wouldn't be any threats on that side of the fort.

A small part of Hemu's troops attacked the fort from the front, while the majority of the troops waited in the rear. While Hemu and his soldiers engaged Mohammad Shah's forces at the main gates, Adnan and the rest of the army swarmed into the fort from the back, taking them by surprise. Attacked from both sides, Mohammad Shah surrendered. Hemu had emerged victorious yet again.

Hemu quelled the rebels at Bayana, Itawa and Narnaul as well. One after the other, victory followed. By now, twenty battles had been successively won by Hemu without any defeat. Adnan became the most-favoured deputy of Hemu, overshadowing Ramaiya.

The next was Chambal Fort occupied by the Mughals.

60

At Chambal Fort, Adnan suggested a novel strategy. Based on this plan, water supply to the fort was first stopped. Attention was then diverted to the gunpowder. The supply of gunpowder to the fort came from outside.

The supplier of the gunpowder was an old trade colleague of Hemu's and had once been a widely preferred vendor for the supply of gunpowder across various kingdoms.

Hemu confiscated the gunpowder in transit and replaced it with a fake powder that resembled gunpowder. It was a powder that did not explode. He made his former trade colleague supply the fake gunpowder to Chambal Fort, occupied by the Mughals.

Hemu deployed his cannons and guns. The cannon wing was ordered to shoot and break the fort walls. The Mughals tried to retaliate using their guns. But their guns did not fire. This offered an easy entry into the fort for Hemu and his team.

The twenty-first battle was won in this way. Adnan's Guruji advised him to always place the mythical axe on top of Hemu's war companion elephant, Hawai. This ensured that no weapon could hurt Hemu. Adnan recalled that the mythical axe could be used only for defence in the Kali Yuga. It could not be used to attack the enemy but could offer protection from the enemy's weapons. Adnan followed this as an established procedure to protect Hemu.

Meanwhile, many things were happening at the Sultanate. There were other Afghans who tried to defy Sultan Adil Shah, one of them being his own brother-in-law, Ibrahim Khan. But Adil Shah challenged him. When Adil Shah reached the Yamuna, Ibrahim Khan sent him a message that he would surrender.

However, when Adil Shah sent his generals for a truce, the generals deserted him and joined Ibrahim Khan. Ibrahim Khan proclaimed himself the sultan of Delhi.

Adil Shah was very sad. He called Hemu.

'Hemu, you see the kind of loyalty these idiots, my own Afghan generals, have towards me. No one can match your vigour, valour and loyalty. I am very happy to have identified you. When the world saw you as a grocer, I saw you as a great warrior and leader.'

'Your Majesty, I will be with you forever. We will destroy all the rebels; do not worry,' Hemu assured Adil Shah.

However, Ibrahim Khan did not rule Delhi for long. He was overthrown by his cousin who took the title Sikandar Shah.

'Hemu, by fighting amongst ourselves, we Afghans are leading ourselves to our own downfall. The empire built by Sher Shah is crumbling. I got a message today, saying that Humayun has defeated Sikandar Shah and occupied Delhi again,' Sultan Adil Shah was very upset. He continued to stay in Chunar and started overseeing Bihar, Bengal and the territories of the Sultanate east of Delhi with Hemu.

'Your Majesty, we shall wait for the right time. We will regain Delhi soon, I promise,' Hemu assured the sultan.

The appropriate time did arrive for Hemu and his team.

61

One day, Hemu asked Adnan to visit a mosque near Agra with Kakkar. An information agent had an important message ready for them. Adnan and Kakkar went to the town near Agra.

'Kakkar, who are these information agents?'

'Adnan, Hemu has set up several sleeper cells in various parts of the region across various kingdoms. They operate as secret sleeper cells, offering us information and helping us raise resources locally during times of war.

'These sleeper cells are in different places: mosques, madrassas, markets, Bhakti and Sufi movement centres and so on. This is the strength of our leader Hemu. He gets qualitative inputs at the right time.'

'Marvellous! I admire our leader,' Adnan was spontaneous in his reaction.

They reached the mosque and entered it for prayers like everyone else.

Asathoo Allah Ilah Illalahoo Vahthahoo Lasary
Kalahoora Asathu anna mahamadan Ahduho!

I am the witness. Allah is my only God. I will never
worship anyone else. I will always obey his orders.
Please make me a clean man.

The prayers were recited by everyone. The assembled men
continued their prayers:

Asathu—Allah—Ilaha—Illalahoova
Achu Anna Mahammad Rasoolillah

After reciting these verses, they ended their prayers by turning
their faces to the right and saying:

Aslamu Alakum Vrahamathulla

Then they turned their faces to the left and said:

Aslamu Alakum Vrahamathulla

The namaz ended. Kakkar went to the mullah of the mosque. The
bearded man had peaceful eyes. He waited for everyone to leave
and called Kakkar to give him a message. It seemed to be the secret
message that Hemu had mentioned, Adnan thought.

Strangely, the mullah called Adnan separately. He asked him,
'Are you a Hindu?'

Adnan was shocked. Does he read people's minds? he
wondered. How could he have asked him such a specific question?

'Why did you ask me this question? I am Adnan; I am a
practising Muslim.'

'I saw you turning your face left when everyone was turning
theirs right and quickly correct yourself. Your mannerism does not
convey conviction to our religious prayers. That is why I asked. You
were so casual. Tell me the truth. I will not harm you. In fact, I

am operating in this identity because of my loyalty to Hemu. I am actually a practising Hindu. You can be honest with me. I opened up to you since you come from Hemu.'

Adnan narrated his story differently without revealing too many details. He told him that his father had been a Brahmin. He was caught by invaders who converted him to Islam. Since he was recently converted, he may have sounded a little odd during the prayer. He claimed to otherwise be a devout Muslim. Adnan did not want anyone to know his true identity, as that would upset Hemu. Hence, he was clear as to what to tell the mullah.

On the other hand, the mullah thought that one day he would meet his lost wife and his children, whom he had lost when he had left his town to protect the precious statues of Chanderi Fort.

Yes, he was none other than Bhargav Ram, the Brahmin pandit, Aditya's father. The father and son met each other, unaware of the other's true identity. Such was the cruelty of destiny.

After receiving the message, both Kakkar and Adnan left for Chunar where Hemu was waiting for them. The secret message was mind-blowing, totally unexpected by both Sultan Adil Shah and Hemu.

....

PART VII

Emperor Vikramaditya Reborn: The Grand Coronation

62

Hemu read the message.

'Humayun has met his death by a fall from the top of the staircase leading to the terraced roof of his library in the palace of Delhi. He lingered for four days, the greater part of the time in a state of senselessness, and expired in the evening of 24 January 1556.

'Tardi Khan Beg, the most eminent of all the nobles of the capital, assumed the general direction of affairs on the spot. His first concern was to conceal the incident from the public until he could arrange to make succession secure for the young Akbar, who was in Punjab with his advisor Bairam Khan. The throne was not declared unoccupied, because an unoccupied throne was a temptation to ambitious people. It created a sense of insecurity and it was feared that the country might plunge into disorder and chaos. For this reason, the emperor's death had to be announced only when a successor had been chosen. A person disguised as Humayun was presented before the public temporarily.

'Somehow, Humayun's death was concealed from the public for seventeen days. On 10 February 1556, the nobles were called to the great mosque, and prayers were recited in the name of Akbar.

'The next act of Tardi Khan Beg was to dispatch the insignia of the empire and the crown jewels, accompanied by the officers of the household and the imperial guards to the headquarters of the new emperor Akbar in Punjab. He was now strengthening the defences against a possible attack by Hemu.

'Meanwhile, fourteen-year-old Akbar was enthroned by Bairam Khan in Kalanaur, Punjab on 14 February 1556. For the coronation, the emperor sat on the throne in the presence of the nobility, the ulema and members of the royal family. Although the coronation usually took place at the capital, it could take place anywhere. Since Akbar was far away from the capital, he had no time to reach it. Hence, the coronation was done on the spot, at Kalanaur, where Akbar was at that time.

'The ceremony was simple. The court and palace had been decorated for the occasion. Poets recited newly composed poems, fireworks were lit for the amusement of people at night, banquets were held and food was distributed among people.

'On accession, many difficulties surrounded Akbar. He made an assessment with his advisor. The throne of Delhi was not secure. Humayun had had no time to stabilize the empire which he had won back very recently before his death. Even Kabul, Kandahar and Badakshan were not safe. The subedar of Badakshan had declared himself independent. Kandahar was always in danger of attack from Persia. In Hindustan, only Delhi and Agra were in the hands of Humayun. The rest of northern Hindustan was with the Afghans. The Rajputs had started reasserting themselves. Above all, the treasury was empty. Revenue could be collected only on the point of the sword and there was widespread famine in the areas near Delhi and Agra. Surrounded by these odds, even the loyalty of Mughal nobility could not be taken for granted.'

The detailed message in the hands of Hemu concluded, 'This is the best time to enter Agra and Delhi.'

The precise details carried confidential information. Adnan admired the remarkable abilities of his leader Hemu in organizing his intelligence team so well.

❧

63

'Hemu, Humayun's successor, Akbar, is only a child. Now is our chance to wipe out the Mughals from this land. You lead the expedition to Delhi and Agra. Come victorious; we will re-establish Sher Shah's empire with all its glories.'

Sultan Adil Shah asked Hemu to proceed without any further delay. Hemu had a quick strategy session with his team.

'Adnan, what is your take on the strategy to capture Agra and Delhi?'

'First, let us talk about Agra. It is better to conserve our forces for more battles and a great fight in Delhi. That will be our twenty-second battle, to be won in succession with not even one failure.'

'Adnan, how do we win Agra without a fight?'

'Did you notice the message which said that the Mughal treasury was empty because of severe famine in the areas surrounding Agra and Delhi?'

'Yes, what is its relevance here?' the ever-hostile Ramaiya chipped in.

'That is the key input for our strategy. You have a number of dedicated sources for grains across various kingdoms. Since Agra and Delhi are starved of grain supply for the Mughal military, they are looking for new sources.

'We can arrange to supply on credit to them, as their treasury is empty. Before sending the grains, we can infuse them with herbs that would gradually de-strengthen people's bones and make them very weak. We should avoid poisoning the grains because the general public may also eat them.'

'Brilliant idea; I shall arrange for it. But who will go to Agra?'

'We can arrange it through the mullah of the mosque who is

operating as your informer. He may add considerable credibility to our offer of grain supply,' Adnan concluded.

The plan worked. The soldiers of Agra Fort became very weak. The Mughal governor of Agra realized that he could not fight with the weak soldiers. The Mughals fled Agra and Hemu could conquer it without a fight.

'Well done, my boys, we conquered Agra without losing any soldiers from our side. We conserved all our resources. We won without striking a single blow, without any boots on the ground. Now we should move for the final assault on Delhi.

'All of you, get ready. We should restore the glory of Sher Shah. This is a do-or-die battle. We should capture Delhi and drive the Mughals out of Hindustan.'

Hemu's powerful speech charged his soldiers. All were ready to move to Delhi.

64

Tardi Khan Beg, the Mughal governor of Delhi, wrote to his masters who were camping at Jalandhar. 'Hemu has captured Agra and intends to attack Delhi. We cannot defend without reinforcements.'

Bairam Khan, the regent of Akbar, realized the gravity of the situation. The main Mughal army could not be spared because of the belligerent presence of other rebels against them. He sent his most capable lieutenant, Pir Muhammad Sharwani, to Delhi. Meanwhile, Tardi Khan Beg ordered all the Mughal nobles in the vicinity to muster forces at Delhi. A council of war was convened, where it was decided that the Mughals would stand and fight Hemu. Plans were made accordingly.

Hemu's camp was fully charged up. He could gather support from both Hindus and Afghans against the Mughals. The Afghans considered themselves to be local sons of the soil and the Mughals as invaders. Hemu also considered the Afghans as local sons of the soil. The unity of the Hindus and the Afghans created a formidable force to take on the Mughals.

At the Mughal court in Delhi, Tardi Khan Beg held consultations with his generals.

'Hemu is on his way with a huge army. He is out to crush us. We cannot defend Delhi. We must retreat to Punjab and join prince Akbar.'

'No, this is not what we are known for. You are asking us to run away even before the enemy is sighted. People will laugh at us. How could we ever face our prince Akbar after running away from here?' Ali Kulf Khan-i-Shibani, one of the commanders, contested the governor's words.

'I know the situation. I give my decision for all of you to follow.

'We will stay here and defend Delhi. But we will keep the lines of retreat open. But, be fully prepared for all eventualities.'

With these words, he concluded the strategy meeting with his generals. The Mughals prepared to fight.

On 6 October 1556, Hemu's twenty-second battle began. For a minute, the number twenty-two crossed Adnan's mind. His Guruji Parasuram had mentioned to him that he would be with him for only twenty-two wars, in which time he should aim to set up a Hindu Raj in Delhi. This reminder alerted him that he should do his best to ensure that Delhi was won at any cost.

65

Hemu and his team reached Tughlaqabad, a village outside Delhi, where they ran into Tardi Khan Beg's forces. The Mughals were outnumbered. Further, the forces of Hemu were reinforced by the arrival of Haji Khan from Alwar.

Hemu's forces comprised a thousand elephants, fifty thousand horses, fifty-one cannons and much more. The troop's formation was a unique one, as conceived by Adnan.

Hemu stayed in the centre with the three hundred best elephants and a force of skilled horsemen. Hemu was sitting on his elephant Hawai. As per the set procedure, Adnan placed the mythical axe on top of Hemu's elephant. He was guarding Hemu from behind. He was waiting for an appropriate moment to spring a surprise attack. The forces on the periphery first engaged the Mughals.

The Mughal army was under the command of Tardi Khan Beg at the centre, Haidar Muhammad on the right and Iskandar Beg on the left. Abdullah Uzbeg commanded the vanguard. The cavalry and left wing attacked Hemu's forces before them. In this assault, the Mughals captured four hundred elephants and slayed three thousand men of Hemu's army. Believing that victory was within reach, many of Tardi Khan Beg's troops dispersed to plunder the enemy camp, leaving him very thinly guarded.

Hemu, who had been silently holding up at the centre, until now not visible to the enemies, seized the opportunity he had been waiting for. He made a sudden and surprising charge at Tardi Khan Beg. At the impetuous advance of the huge beasts and dense cavalry behind them, many of the Mughal officers fled in terror without waiting to offer a defence. In the end, Tardi Khan Beg himself took the same course.

When the previously victorious Mughal vanguard and left wing returned from their pursuit, they realized that the day was lost and dispersed without putting up a fight. Delhi fell into the hands of Hemu on 7 October 1556. The Mughals were routed.

❧

66

Chants of 'Long live Hemu!' rent the sky. All the Mughal wealth fell into Hemu's hands.

'Distribute the booty among all the soldiers. Those who were willing to die for the king should get all the rewards,' Hemu ordered liberal distribution of the captured wealth. He made a grand entry into the palace. At that time, a loud cry arose, 'Raja Hemu ki Jai!' started by Adnan. Then everyone followed him. 'Raja Hemu Ki Jai!'

Hemu could see Adnan, his favourite deputy. 'Adnan could read my inner mind. He is spot-on. I have been very closely guarding my ambition of setting up a Hindu Raj. The scars I received on the battlefield always reminded me to move towards my goal of a Hindu Raj. I dedicate this victory to the innumerable men and women, the ordinary sons and daughters of the soil, who showed extraordinary conviction in defending our tradition, culture and dignity.

'The Afghans are fighting amongst themselves, and I toiled to reach this day. I shall proclaim myself king and form a Hindu Raj. Why not? Success happens when talent meets opportunity. Opportunity is now knocking at my door. I should not miss it.'

Hemu had made up his mind. He decided to claim royal status

and assume the title of Vikramaditya, an appellation which had been used by many Hindu kings in the ancient past.

The coronation ceremony followed soon. It took place at Purana Qila in Delhi on a grand scale.

67

The Rajyabhishek or coronation followed all Hindu rituals. Hemu sat on the royal throne and assumed the title of Raja Vikramaditya. He wanted to model his state on the lines of the famous Vijayanagar empire of the south.

After three hundred and fifty years of almost unbroken rule by invaders, a son of the soil was being crowned that day. It was a proud moment.

The coronation ceremony was attended by more than fifty thousand people. The Afghan nobles and commanders were also present. They celebrated the event as though one among them had become the ruler. There was unanimous acceptance of Hemu, even among the Afghans, as they liked the way he led them from the front and the way he magnanimously distributed the captured wealth. They also knew that Afghan sultans fought each other. Only Hemu could provide a safe government and destroy other invaders.

The Afghans considered themselves to be sons of the soil like Hemu, united against outsiders like the Mughal invaders.

Many Hindu rituals and prayers were conducted by the chief priest of Kasi, who came with a team of over a hundred Vedic pandits. Many Brahmin priests also attended.

Diplomats from various states, including the Rajput states, the Vijayanagar empire, the Naiks from the south and the governors of Bihar and Bengal came to pay their respects to Hemu.

Hemu distributed fine pieces of cloth and several other things among the Brahmin pandits who came to bless him. He took his seat on a gold-plated royal throne decked with ornaments. His queen sat on his left and his close aides, Ramaiya, Kakkar, Haji Khan and Adnan, stood close behind him. The Vedic pandits stood with golden jugs full of water from the sacred rivers Narmada, Sindhu, Kaveri and Ganges, and poured them over the head of the king. The Rajyabhishek ceremony was accompanied by music.

Brahmin ladies with lamps on golden trays waved the light around the king's head. Hemu then changed into a royal scarlet robe and wore precious ornaments.

He worshipped the weapons put on display there and bowed to his elders: his father, uncles and all the nobles and dignitaries assembled there. He then took his seat on the throne.

Chants of 'Long live Raja Vikramaditya!' echoed all around the palace. The priest held the royal umbrella over his head and hailed him as Raja Vikramaditya.

'Long live Raja Vikramaditya!' the crowd roared again. Salvos of shots were fired at the exact same time from all the forts in the kingdom.

After the grand Rajyabhishek ceremony, Raja Vikramaditya began his speech. The royal hall fell silent as he commenced speaking.

68

'Let me make it clear. Our state will be a Hindu Raj, which means that it will be a confluence of nationalism and patriotism.

'It will be a secular Raj where there will be welfare for all and appeasement of none. This will be a kingdom that will operate only on the basis of rewarding meritocracy and performance. It will be a Ram Rajya, where every citizen of our soil will get fair and just treatment, with no discrimination based on caste, creed or colour.

'It will follow the Upanishad's words, which have been ingrained in our civilization for thousands of years. "Ekam Sat Vipra Bahudha Vadanti." The truth is one but we call it different names.

'Hindu Raj stands for secular Raj, as we believe in respecting everyone's faith. All paths lead to one destination, God. We pursue polytheism, worship multiple deities and hence, there is no place for hatred for any form of worship by anyone.

'Yes, the Hindu community has suffered many atrocities over three hundred years. We have two options: either we show love and win over the people of other faiths who made us suffer such atrocities, or hate them and retaliate.

'I appeal to all of you to pursue the path of love for all, which will be the state's policy.

'I should confess something at this stage. I hail from a poor family. I was not born a Kshatriya or a royal. It is only my Afghan ruler and Afghan brothers who brought me on this great journey. To confess honestly, had I been in a Hindu kingdom all along, I would have only seen a palace from a distance, and could have never dreamt of occupying it.

'I am grateful to my Afghan brothers and nobles for having

faith in me. Therefore, I will not do anything that disturbs the communal harmony between Hindus and Muslims. We co-exist peacefully. We may not forget the atrocities committed on us very easily, but we must see these as scars that remind us to never repeat such atrocities in future.

'Many of my Hindu friends who take extreme positions requested me to levy an Islamic tax, while repealing the jizya tax or Hindu tax. I assure you that there will not be any tax that would discriminate against you based on your beliefs.

'We have to fight only foreign invaders. It is now a fight between invaders and local citizens of our soil. It is not a fight between Islam and Hinduism. Our Afghan brothers are the sons of this soil. They practise Islam. But nothing can take away their patriotism for this soil. They shed their blood in the war against Mughals. Our main enemies are the Mughals, the foreign invaders.

'I conclude with these words: I am not your ruler; I am your prime sevak.

'Now we move on to award titles to the various achievers of our kingdom.'

As Raja Hemu concluded his speech, there was a standing ovation from all those present, Afghans and Hindus.

69

Many titles and awards were to be announced next. Ramaiya was to become the head of cavalry; Haji Khan, the head of archery; Shadi Khan Kakkar, the head of infantry, and so on. Many Afghan nobles were to be given jagirs: the right to collect revenue in their territories. Gallantry awards to brave soldiers were also lined up. Above all, Hemu wanted to assign the role of prime minister to the young Adnan who was merely twenty-eight years old.

Hemu decided to elevate him since he felt that Adnan was the architect of many of his victories. He had a strategic mind and 'try anything' spirit and brought creative value addition every time.

Ramaiya, his nephew, was angry when Hemu shared this information with him confidentially. He did not conceal his anger. Hemu promised him that he would make him the chief commander of the army soon. Only then was Ramaiya pacified. But Adnan had not yet been informed of this. Hemu wanted it to be a surprise.

The announcement had to be made after the personal visits of diplomats and dignitaries who paid respects to the king with gifts.

At this hour, a surprise visitor walked in and that destroyed the happiness of King Hemu. His sister, Meera, who had walked out of his house three decades ago now walked in, towards him.

'Why is she here? How is she here?' Hemu was angry.

At that very moment, Adnan received her and took her to Hemu.

'Sorry, uncle, I concealed my identity all along. I am Aditya, Meera's son, your nephew. I wanted to unite you with my mother, who is your sister. I thought the best way was to assist you, to establish a Hindu Raj and then bring her to you.'

'What nonsense! I do not want to meet anyone who walked out of my house. She did exactly the opposite of what we wanted her to do. Do you think my anger has died? I can pardon anyone but not her. Now I do not pardon you, you cheat. You concealed your identity for so long!' Hemu thundered. The whole gathering watched the scene in complete silence.

'To avoid provoking your anger, I joined with a camouflaged identity. I wanted to reveal my identity after achieving the goal of setting up a Hindu Raj, as per my Guruji's directions.'

'What? You assisted me in forming a Hindu Raj?'

'Yes, I was guided by my Guruji, Ramdas, who taught me

martial arts and gave me his mythical axe to protect you. Only with these could I ensure your victories.'

'Shut up and get out. I gained these victories with my hardworking army men, both Afghans and Hindustanis. You are making their efforts sound trivial by attributing these victories to some Guruji and his axe. What rubbish! Had someone else done this, I would have killed him on the spot. You are lucky. As I am being crowned today, I do not want to sentence anyone.

'You and your mother should leave this kingdom immediately. If you stay here, I will imprison both of you. Leave immediately!'

The whole crowd witnessed the anger of their king from close quarters.

Ramaiya giggled. He told King Hemu in a low voice, 'I kept warning you about Adnan, sorry, Aditya.'

Both Meera and Aditya left the place with eyes full of tears. The man who could have become prime minister in a short while was labelled a traitor. This is fate, Aditya thought.

Meanwhile, the announcement of awards was completed and the coronation ceremony came to a conclusion. The announcement about Aditya was withheld.

PART VIII

....

The Mother of All Battles

70

Aditya took his mother back home. He asked her why she had paid such a surprise visit. He could have taken some time to explain things to Hemu so that his anger would have subsided.

'My son, your foster uncle Abdul Gafoor sent me here. He told me that you had become very close to your uncle Hemu. He said that I shouldn't miss Hemu's coronation today and made arrangements for my visit. He told me to make it a surprise for you too,' Meera explained.

'I understand. He might have thought that all would end well. But I had not yet revealed my identity. I thought I would slowly reveal my identity after the coronation,' Aditya exclaimed, grieved.

'Mother, I had planned on uniting the two of you. That is why I went through all this trouble. But now things have gone out of control. We have reached an irreconcilable stage. I'm sorry.'

'My son, you cannot do anything about this. This is our destiny. I am unable to be with my brother or my husband, for whom I had walked out of the house,' Meera could not control her tears.

Aditya visited Ameer Chishti, the Sufi saint, to seek refuge at his centre, as he had to vacate the house. The Sufi centre gave asylum to Aditya, his wife and his mother. Aditya realized that his Guruji no longer appeared at his request. His mythical axe had also vanished. He understood that this was because the twenty-two wars were over and because he had told Hemu about his Guruji and the mythical axe.

A few weeks passed. Hemu brought about several changes to the army, including the recruitment of many Hindustanis, but without the dismissal of any Afghan.

Further, because of his long association with the Sher Shah administration for over a decade, Hemu had great experience in administration and sound knowledge of how the system worked. He revitalized the administration that had weakened after the demise of Sher Shah Suri. With his knowledge of trade and commerce, he gave fresh impetus to commerce throughout the country. He did not spare anyone who indulged in blackmarketing, hoarding, overcharging and underweighting of goods. He replaced all the corrupt officers.

He introduced coinage bearing his name. He declared meritocracy and performance alone as the criteria for promotions and engagement. He revamped the education system of the country to make it more performance-centric. Religion, caste, creed and colour took a backseat.

Within a month, the changes were so palpable that all sections of society could feel a secular Hindu Raj governing them.

He introduced radical social reforms, abolishing sati in his state and presenting new alternatives for widows to live with dignity. He also abolished the triple talaq to protect Muslim women from being divorced without any compensation.

While all the changes brought about by him were unanimously praised, the radical social reforms caused dissent among some fanatic followers of the respective religions. This dissent gradually built enemies for Hemu from within. These disgruntled elements from either religion tried to establish contact with invaders and rebels to topple Hemu from the throne. Meanwhile, Akbar's camp had other plans.

71

When Akbar heard of Hemu's success, he assembled his warrior nobles and asked them for advice. All of them urged him to fall back on Kabul and move away from the fiery warrior Hemu. They were of the opinion that Akbar was too young. He could grow up, buy time and then attack Hemu with large forces. There was a single dissenting voice. It was a powerful voice for an immediate attack on Hemu without further delay. He said that Delhi was the decisive point, not Kabul. This was the voice of Bairam Khan.

The instincts of Akbar matched the advice of Bairam Khan. They decided to go ahead with the plan. A march across Sutlej was ordered. Both of them felt that if Hemu was allowed to consolidate at Delhi, he may even attack Kabul later.

All of them crossed the Sutlej and captured the town of Srihand. Akbar was joined there by Tardi Khan Beg and the other nobles who had been defeated by Hemu at Delhi. Tardi Khan Beg was a Turkish nobleman who had shifted his allegiance between Humayun and his brothers a couple of times and finally sided with Humayun.

When Humayun died, it was Tardi Khan Beg who had arranged the bloodless succession to Akbar. His loyalty was unquestionable, but his hasty evacuation of Delhi against Hemu had been a tactical blunder. However, it had not been an intentional crime against the Sultanate.

But Bairam Khan and Tardi Khan Beg were professional rivals and a growing jealousy had always been the hallmark of their relationship. Beyond this, there were religious differences between them, for Bairam Khan belonged to the Shia division of Islam while

Tardi Khan Beg belonged to the Sunni sect. Bairam, who was now the advisor of Akbar, thought it was time to eliminate Tardi Khan Beg to avoid any nobles contesting his growth. He summoned Tardi Khan Beg to his tent and assassinated him on the spot.

Akbar was displeased with this act, but Bairam Khan excused himself on the grounds that such an act was necessary in the interest of discipline, to secure the subordination of the nobles.

Akbar started moving towards Panipat from Srihand. But before that, he had taken the precaution to dispatch in advance a force of ten thousand horsemen, under the command of Ali Kuli Khan. He was the same general who had condemned Tardi Khan Beg for the hasty withdrawal from Delhi. At this hour, Hemu was getting ready with a different approach.

72

Hemu had a surprise visitor. Someone called Yusuf Khan, claiming to be the son of Tardi Khan Beg, the noble who was killed by Bairam Khan.

'What is the need for a Mughal noble's son to visit me?' Hemu wondered. His new minister chipped in.'Your Majesty, an enemy's enemy is our friend. Very recently, his father was killed by Bairam Khan, Akbar's advisor. Bairam Khan settled scores with Tardi Khan Beg since he was potential threat. Moreover, Tardi Khan Beg belonged to the Sunni sect, not the Shia sect of Bairam Khan. This act was committed against Tardi Khan Beg for running away from Delhi when you invaded.'

Hemu asked Yusuf Khan, 'Therefore, you turned against Bairam

Khan and Akbar? How do I believe you?'

'Your Majesty, why should I come all the way to you? I carry vital information for you.'

'What is it?'

'Your Majesty, Akbar is planning to invade Delhi. He wants to take you on at a battlefield in Panipat, where his grandfather had defeated Ibrahim Lodi. They may start the war in one month. But before they arrive, I suggest you place your forces in Panipat well in advance, Your Majesty.'

'You gave me a good intelligence input. I will move my forces tomorrow itself.'

'Move your artillery first to seize the opportunity, Your Majesty. Moving the artillery ahead of the main force will enable you to be ready for war as you move in. The artillery moves very slowly, and if it comes along with the main forces, you will be delayed, Your Majesty.'

'What do you think, Ramaiya?'

'Your Majesty, what he says is right. However, our artillery head, Haji Khan, is currently in Chambal, dealing with the rebels. He may take some time to get here.'

'So what? We shall send the artillery with minimum security as it is only a movement now. There are no threats from any enemy until Akbar arrives at Panipat. We need not wait for Haji Khan and delay the process. Let us move the artillery at least with the weak guards, Mubarak Khan and Bahadur Khan. No need to have a lot of protection for the artillery since it may take us some more time to get our forces into Delhi.'

The heavy artillery normally had to move first. It had to be carried on ox-drawn or elephant-drawn carts, or in extreme cases, even pushed physically to their deployment areas. Hundreds of labourers had to march with spades, ready to smoothen the ground over which the artillery moved. Hence, Hemu thought it better to send the artillery in advance, with only the labour force and minimal protection at that stage when the threat of attack was low. Further, the main forces moved fast and they could catch up with the artillery quickly, even if they started late.

'Your Majesty, if you don't have any objections, I can accompany the artillery and will provide support should any exigency arise. Even if any Mughal force comes, I can handle the situation, as they all think I am still a part of the Mughal army,' Yusuf Khan said.

'Very good, Yusuf Khan. Move with our artillery today itself. I will meet you soon at Panipat with my army. Let us make our battle positions to our advantage by reaching Panipat much earlier than Akbar.'

Hemu's artillery was equipped with the best gunpowder, recently acquired from Turkish traders. The entire artillery was moved out of Delhi, as Hemu thought that the best artillery of his army would settle the war in his favour. He decided to use his artillery as his unique strength.

Within a day, the heavy artillery moved out of Delhi as planned. As discussed, Yusuf Khan also accompanied them. Raja Hemu later understood how grave a mistake he had made in sending his artillery without protection.

73

Raja Hemu's artillery moved slower than it usually did. Yusuf Khan was guiding them. Suddenly, hundreds of horsemen headed by the Mughal commander Ali Kuli Khan appeared. Mubarak Khan wondered how the Mughals were there, well before them.

'Did Yusuf Khan lie to us that the Mughals would reach only after a month?' he thought.

His doubt was resolved soon. Yusuf Khan greeted Ali Kuli Khan.

'Welcome to the world of Raja Hemu. I knew you would rebel against Akbar because of the heightened domination of Bairam Khan. Join us; I am now guiding the artillery forces of Raja Hemu.'

Mubarak Khan was happy to receive the horsemen on their side. There were fast-moving Arabian horses with swift archers commanding them.

These horsemen joined Raja Hemu's artillery. Since Yusuf Khan was given freedom to command the artillery forces, all of them moved towards Panipat together.

Unfortunately, that night Mubarak Khan and Bahadur Khan, the commanders belonging to Raja Hemu, were murdered, and the entire artillery was converted to that of the Mughal forces.

Meanwhile, Yusuf Khan was celebrating the occasion.

'That idiot Hemu was very well foxed by us. He easily believed my story completely and gifted his best artillery to us. He does not have the gunpowder which he carefully stocked by importing from the Sultanate of Turkey.'

The complete artillery force was lost. This news shook Hemu's army commanders.

'What? That Yusuf Khan was a cheat? It is a major blow to our army, uncle!'

'Ramaiya, do not worry. The world does not end with the artillery. We have won many times before without engaging the artillery. Our elephant and horse forces will win the war for us.

'But I have to admit that the absence of the brilliance of Adnan is being felt. He would not hesitate to challenge and apply brakes to my rash decisions. I am definitely missing him at this critical hour.'

'Uncle, you still have that cheat on your mind. He may be

intelligent, but he is not loyal. I received further intelligence about his background. He and his mother were under the care of a Mughal commander in the Punjab region. We were feeding milk to a poisonous snake.'

'Yes, I know that. But my sister who was once loved by our family so much would definitely not go to the extent of spying on me for my enemy. Ours was only a family rivalry.'

'Uncle, you were once very close to your sister Meera, showering all your affection on her even at the cost of denying my mother her share of affection. She was your other sister, but your love and affection for Meera was very deep. You still do not give her up from your memory.'

'Ramaiya, I have done enough for you. I have given power, position and status to you. But I have completely denounced my sister Meera. Even her son was liked by me only because of his performance and not because of our blood relationship. But I still do not approve of the way she walked out of our house, ignoring our family prestige and tradition. Anyway, let us not recall family memories now when we have a great national duty ahead of us to protect our Hindu Raj from the foreign invaders.

'Let us assemble the forces. We will all move with our best army with which I won twenty-two wars in succession. I will lead the forces myself. By tomorrow, we leave Delhi and reach Panipat quickly. The invaders have already reached. Focus on the movement of troops; forget the family issues now. Consider this my order as the chief commander of the forces of this Hindu Raj.'

Raja Hemu was firm in his directions.

74

The decisive battle was fought on 5 November 1556 on a plain near Panipat.

The Mughal army had a massive twenty-thousand-strong cavalry. The artillery, along with Hemu's captured forces, also lent its full support. Sikandar Khan Uzbek commanded the right wing, while the left was under Abdulla Khan Uzbek. Ali Quli Khan Shaibani had control of the centre, while the vanguard was led by Husain Quli Beg and Sha Quli Mahram. Akbar and Bairam Khan did not participate in the battle and were safely ensconced in the Mughal camp, several miles away from the battlefield.

Hemu advanced to Panipat, leading thirty thousand strong Rajput and Afghan horsemen, comrades of earlier victories. Only Adnan was missing amongst them. He had five hundred war elephants, protected by plate armour, who carried musketeers and crossbowmen. The commanders were men of valour and loyalty and proud of their past deeds. But Hemu had no field guns, as they had fallen into Mughal hands prior to the battle. Hemu did not bother about that major loss. He was confident of winning the battle even without his guns. Hemu took a position in the centre, on his favourite elephant Hawai. The right wing was commanded by Shadi Khan Kakkar, and the left wing by Ramaiya.

The vanguard was under the command of Hemu's brother Bhawan Das.

The battle positions were drawn up like this:

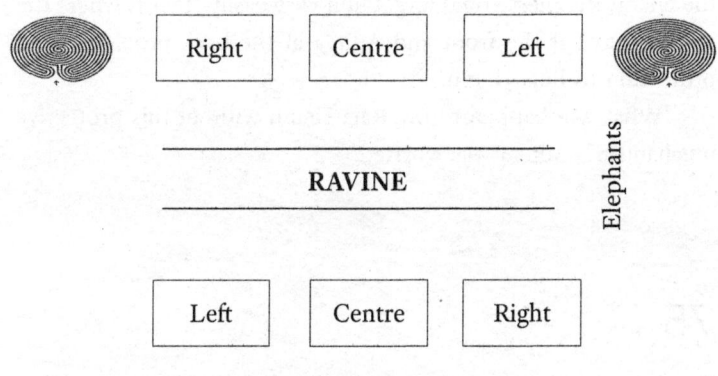

Akbar's forces

| Right | Centre | Left |

RAVINE

Elephants

| Left | Centre | Right |

Hemu's forces

The Mughals took a defensive position in front of a deep ravine. Neither Hemu's elephants nor his horse units were able to cross the chasm to reach their opponents and were vulnerable to the projectile weapons being fired from the other side.

A serious battle was on.

Meanwhile, Aditya came to know that the artillery forces had simply been taken away from Hemu because of his tactical blunder. He felt very sorry for not being able to accompany Raja Hemu at that critical hour. Further, he was also worried that the mythical axe which had protected Hemu from the top of his elephant Hawai was not with him now.

Hemu, in all the twenty-two wars that he had won, had always been protected by the mythical axe placed in front of him, on top of his elephant, while at the back Adnan would protect him as an impregnable defence wall. Now since both were missing, Aditya was worried.

From atop the elephant, Hemu would always get the best view and could give commands sitting there. Hence, he always preferred sitting on top of the elephant. But this position was also risky as the enemy's archers could target him very easily. That is where the mythical axe at the front and Aditya at the back provided solid protection to Raja Hemu.

'What will happen to my Raja Hemu without this protective mechanism?' Aditya was worried.

∽

75

Raja Hemu's forces took the initiative. The assault of the elephants shook the right and left wings of the Mughal army and many of their warriors fell. The survivors did not flee, but withdrew to the flanks in order to avoid being hit by the elephants. The wings then assailed Hemu's cavalry, making a detour and attacking the enemy horsemen's flanks. The Mughals also harassed Hemu's forces with their superior archery.

The Mughal centre wing also advanced but encountered the shallow ravine in front, which was impassable for the elephants. It therefore adopted a defensive posture and continued to engage Hemu's army with arrows.

Ali Quli Khan devised an ingenious plan to attack Hemu. He sent his archers, who, in turn, were protected by swordsmen, to encircle the centre and attempt to get closer to Hemu. As the formation got closer to the target, they fired volley after volley of arrows towards Hemu.

Meanwhile, the cavalry of the Mughal army managed to penetrate Hemu's army from the flanks and the rear. As Hemu's army's attack reduced in intensity and the elephants fell back, Ali

Quli Khan sailed forward with his cavalry, made a detour and attacked Hemu's army's centre from the rear.

Hemu, who was surveying the battlefield and directing the operations aloft his elephant, hastened to the threatened sector in an endeavour to restore the situation. He directed repeated counterattacks with his powerful elephants, pushing back the Mughals in the direct line of his advance.

But the battle was taking its toll. The best of Hemu's generals were killed. Shadi Khan Kakkar was trampled to death, while Bhawan Das, a gallant general, was cut to pieces. Similarly, Khwaja Kakkar, the father of Shadi Khan, Mahmud Khan Lodi and Qasim Khan Lodi were also slain.

Raja Hemu could not continue as a mere spectator and he put in his best efforts to stem the tide. He conceived numerous strategies and dislodged many strong soldiers of the Mughal army. That made the battle more fierce and bloody.

The death of his generals, right in front of his eyes, did not deter Hemu. As a true Karma Yogi, he went on striving for the best. His act of bravery inspired his troops and they all fought desperately to turn the tide of the battle in their favour. Hemu's forces felt that victory was within reach.

Alas, a random arrow flew in and pierced Hemu's eyes at that crucial moment. However, that did not dampen the spirits of the great warrior Hemu. Soldiers near him could see blood spouting from the wound. But he pulled the arrow out, bandaged his eye with a scarf and ordered his soldiers to continue fighting. This was a rare act of bravery and courage, nowhere heard of in any battlefield in history.

76

The wound on Raja Hemu's eye was serious. The grievousness of the wound caused him to collapse unconscious on his elephant. The fall of the leader caused his Afghan-Rajput army to panic.

The favourite elephant of Raja Hemu ran away, carrying him from the battlefield to the forests located on the banks of the Yamuna. The loyal elephant wanted to carry her master away, to get him treated at a herbal clinic located in the middle of the jungle.

Meanwhile, news spread amongst Raja Hemu's army that their leader had been killed by the Mughals. The battle ended as Raja Hemu's forces surrendered upon hearing the news of their leader's death.

However, Raja Hemu was fighting the battle for his life. Meanwhile, Aditya learnt of the developments and was deeply distressed. His wondered how his leader, a strong fighter who had won twenty-two battles in succession, could be defeated by Akbar's army.

He realized that a few issues had not favoured Raja Hemu.

First, Raja Hemu had committed a tactical blunder in allowing his artillery to be captured so easily by the Mughals. This was because of the reliance on the false intelligence about the movement of Akbar's troops.

Second, Raja Hemu's troops were not steadfast in the battle and there was no one to take control of the army after the arrow hit Raja Hemu. The soldiers thought that their leader had been killed and hence fled the battlefield. There was no other leader who could motivate them to fight.

Third, the superior cavalry and archery of the Mughals

confused and demoralized Raja Hemu's soldiers.

Like Akbar and Bairam Khan, Raja Hemu should have stayed away from the battle. He should have let his generals fight first while staying in the background. That would have given him an opportunity for a second attack and would have avoided demoralizing his forces. But the social conditioning of the Rajput society is to take the fight head-on; it offered no possibility of a tactical withdrawal or temporary losses. Whenever the prospect of victory faded, morale was crushed.

Finally, enforceable accidents in the course of a battle tended to preclude the best result, more so when a commander lost the ability to communicate with others. Had the arrow not hit Raja Hemu and had he survived for a few more hours, he would have destroyed Akbar's forces, who were on the backfoot at the time of the accident.

But where had the arrow come from? Who shot the arrow? Was Raja Hemu dead or alive? These questions bothered Aditya.

While he was seeking answers to these introspective questions, a messenger hurriedly came to Aditya with an urgent message from Raja Hemu.

'Adnan, sorry, my dearest nephew Aditya, rush and come immediately with the messenger. I think I am in the final stages of my life. Before I breathe my last, I want to talk to you urgently and assign you the unfinished task. Come immediately!'—Raja Hemu.

Aditya immediately rushed to see his leader Raja Hemu, as per the instructions.

PART IX

....

The Aftermath

77

The wind was blowing softly, releasing a breath of fresh air. The birds were chirping sweetly. The gentle breeze rustled the leaves. The leaves seemed to be desperate to fall off the tree and join their companions on the forest floor.

The grass tickled the bare feet and gentle dewdrops fell from the leaves onto the forehead. A sweet smell coming from the flowers wafted through the air. In the midst of the green trees, there was a hut with herbal medicines within.

Aditya reached the place where he saw Raja Hemu lying on his deathbed, his elephant guarding him. A doctor was applying some herbal paste around the wounds.

'Welcome, Aditya. I have limited time at my disposal. Hence, listen to me carefully.'

'Yes, Your Majesty.'

'Call me Uncle.'

'Yes, Uncle.'

'I did hold my anger against your mother for a long time. Later, I saw the invaders crushing us. When the invader attacked our religion, tradition and culture, I wondered why we were not coming together as a Hindu community as a whole.

'When I was a trader living in a small town focusing on my trade, unaffected by the foreign Islamic invaders, I did not realize the importance of unity amongst Hindus. I was a caste fanatic until I directly faced the atrocities committed by these Islamic invaders.

'Before the invaders came, within our land, we had kings who were invading other kingdoms for expansion. But when these invaders came to our land, they not only expanded their kingdom but also tried to destroy our tradition, culture, religion, dignity and pride. Hence, Hindus had to unite against foreign invaders. That was the time I felt the need for Hindu unity. I tried to understand our Hindu religion. The Varna was not birth-based and was only a division of labour to achieve specialization. The great rishis who gave us the *Ramayana* and *Mahabharata* were not Brahmins by birth. They were recognized as Brahmins by their deeds.

'The Vedas did say that God was shapeless. The saying that the Brahmins came from the mouth and Kshatriyas came from the arms of the God is a divisive statement. How can a shapeless God, as defined by the Vedas, say that each sect is from a different part of the body? The verse of Purusha Sukta, which defined such status, only stated this:

"Visualizing the God as the whole planet, the Brahmins are assumed to be the mouth (representing reciting of the Vedas) the Kshatriyas, the arms (representing warrior skills) the Vaishyas, the thigh (representing the money flow which forms the pillar of the economy) and the rest, the Shudras, are the feet (representing their lending assistance to all others)..."

'I came to understand that the issue was not one of hierarchy, but that of classification. Hinduism never had any system of slavery unlike the invaders' religion. I also noted that there are class conflicts within Islam: Sunni versus Shia, Ameer versus Gulami and so on. When the Shudras are said to be visualized as the feet, there is no offense intended. The Advaita philosophy of Hinduism goes further to say that there are no differences between caste, creed, religion and gender, since we are all manifestations of the same Brahman, the God. Even the environment, the trees, plants and animals are considered an extension of God. The *Rig Veda* says, 'A trader is like a honey bee who sucks honey from the flower without damaging the beauty and fragrance of the flower.'

In the same way, it says that we need to live without damaging the environment. Our religion considered even the environment as Vasu Deva Kutumbum. I realized all this much later, when I faced the onslaught of the invading Mughals against our Hindus.

'I realized I had been too harsh to my sister, your mother, when she married a Brahmin outside our caste, much against the wishes of our family. But when I realized my mistake, it was too late. Your mother had reached the enemy's state, beyond my reach. Her joining my enemy completely alienated her from me. Your mother did not want to see me at all; her anger against me was much more than mine.

'In fact, your father, Bhargav Ram, worked for me on a secret mission.'

'Is that so? Where is he?'

Aditya could not control his excitement.

78

'Yes, Aditya, your father is still working as a sleeper cell, giving me intelligence inputs by working as a mullah in a mosque. For the sake of creating a Hindu Raj, he safely deposited the sacred idols in a secret location, converted to Islam and created a fake identity. You met him once in a mosque near Agra.'

'Yes, uncle. Oh my God! We spoke to each other, unaware of the relationship we shared.'

'Like him, there are many such sleeper cells working for us in different places. I was always nourishing the ambition of creating a Hindu Raj. But I first wanted to rise in stature in the Sultanate, without giving the sultans opportunities to doubt me. I wanted to declare a Hindu Raj once I consolidated my position. I eventually did.

'In fact, I wanted to make you my prime minister. But too many things happened and we parted ways.

'The great Muslim Afghan generals died while defending this nation. They are sons of the soil unlike the foreign Mughal invaders. But my own nephew Ramaiya shot the arrow that pierced my eyes. I failed to recognize the enemy within. He walked away to the opposition camp at the crucial hour, with many of our soldiers, for some promised rewards. I learnt from my sources that you were in Delhi. That is why I called you.'

'What are the tasks for me? Please tell me. I am even ready to die for you, uncle.'

'Yes, I called you to tell you your tasks. Acharya Chanakya said, "Even if a snake is not poisonous, he should pretend to be venomous in order to survive." Similarly, Hindus may not try to convert others, but when attacked, they have to counterattack, combining as a massive community. Hence, you have to unite the Hindus and create a Virat Hindu community. You have to save my father, your grandfather and other men and women loyal to me, both Hindus and Afghan Muslims who are hiding in a secret place near the fort. You must save them from the ill treatment of Mughals. My father is eighty years old; I do not want him to be harmed at any cost.

'Unite the forces, re-establish the Hindu Raj and let your command restore the pride of the Vikramaditya rule, which I created only a month ago. Drive the Mughals out of our land and create a Hindu Raj, a secular Raj that serves its best to all with appeasement to none. All religions, castes, creeds and colours will co-exist peacefully in our new Raj to be re-established by you.

'You can, you will. You do not know your capability, Aditya, but I do.'

'But uncle, I cannot leave you in this condition. I am also not able to digest the fact that our own family member shot an arrow into your eyes.'

'No, Aditya, your duty towards the nation calls you now. You have a considerable distance to traverse in the journey of your life. Do not worry about me. Leave immediately to fulfil the duty assigned to you by your king. This is Raja Hemu's last order in his life.

'Before I breathe my last, I will give you this advice. Once you rule the Hindu Raj,

be a lovable person, but don't become a slave;
be sympathetic, but don't get cheated;
be humble, but don't be a coward;
be stubborn, but don't be angry;
be cautious in spending, but don't be a miser;
be a brave man, but don't be a bad man;
be busy, but don't get perturbed;
be dharmic, but don't become bankrupt;
be wealth conscious, but don't be greedy;
be compassionate to all, but appease none.

'Aditya, I once denounced you since your mother married a Brahmin pandit. I thought the son born to that Brahmin would be timid and would accept the ill treatment of opponents as karma without opposing it.

'You proved me wrong. I realized that your father dedicated his life to a national cause and that you proved to be a great warrior. Who says a Brahmin cannot be a Virat Hindu?' You are a Virat Hindu Brahmin warrior, of the Hindu secular Raj of Hemu. The term Brahmin warrior may have, until now, been considered an oxymoron, as a Brahmin and a warrior are mutually exclusive, contradictory words. Henceforth, it will be an accepted term because your valour will prove its usage correct.

'From my deathbed, I hereby confer the title "Brahmin Warrior" on you.

'Goodbye, Brahmin Warrior, may victory be yours!'

Reluctantly, Aditya left the place to attend to the new task assigned to him by his ruler.

✧

79

Aditya rushed to the mosque near the palace. The mullah of the mosque was also a sleeper cell of Raja Hemu. Hemu's aged father, wife, relatives and many of his loyal guards had taken refuge in the mosque.

All of them thought that they would be safe in a mosque managed by a mullah close to Raja Hemu. The Mughals may not attack the mosque, they thought. Aditya reached the mosque according to the instructions of his leader Hemu. He had to save its inhabitants and move them out of Delhi to a safe place quickly.

When Aditya reached the mosque, he saw the mullah of the mosque near Agra, whom he had met earlier. He recognized him as his father, based on what he had been told by Raja Hemu. He went to him and said that he was his son Aditya, operating under a secret identity as Adnan.

The mullah, his father Bhargav Ram, embraced him with tears in his eyes.

'What a way to meet my son after twenty-eight years. I cannot talk to you for long, as we are running short of time. I am happy that I could at least meet you during my lifetime. Tell me about the plan now.'

Aditya unveiled the plan.

'All of you listen carefully. Hemu's father and my grandfather ...' he started.

'Grandfather?' the eighty-year-old father of Raja Hemu exclaimed.

'Yes, fate separated us. My mother Meera walked out of your house on her marriage. Meet my father, your son-in-law Bhargav Ram, whom you have never met until now.

'Our karma forced us to meet at a time of crisis, when Raja Hemu is on his deathbed. I am executing the instructions given by my uncle, Raja Hemu.'

'Here is the plan. All of you will go with my father who is now known as the mullah of a mosque near Agra. He will not be disturbed by the Mughal army since he is an Islamic priest.

'All the women, including Raja Hemu's queen, have to wear a burka and get ready to move.

'All the men will have to recite the Islamic verses as taught by my father and move as a caravan towards Agra. From there, arrangements will be made to travel to Bundelkhand, our neighbouring kingdom. Is everything clear?'

'I am eighty years old, I do not have the desire to live longer. I am ready to face the consequences here. Why should I hide myself? I am the father of the brave Raja Hemu. I am not leaving Delhi,' Hemu's father was firm.

All the Afghan generals loyal to Hemu also refused. They wanted to fight until death, rather than run away from there.

Even Raja Hemu's wife refused. But Aditya pleaded with her, saying that he would not like her to lose her dignity. Hence, she should not stay and face the brutal Mughals.

After considerable deliberation, it was agreed that all the men would stay back and that the women would go to Agra escorted by Aditya's father. They all moved, leaving the men behind.

As soon as they left, the mullah of the Delhi mosque went to Aditya, stating that they had to vacate the place within a day. The Mughals were taking over the mosques in Delhi and hence the men who sought shelter there had to leave.

Aditya had to quickly find a solution. He thought of seeking shelter at the Sufi centre of Ameer Chishti. He rushed there. To his surprise, he met his foster uncle Abdul Gafoor and his mother Meera there.

Meera was briefed about the situation. She could not control her emotions when she learnt of the fate that had befallen her brother and her aged father. After all, one's blood relationships never get diluted even after the bitterest fights.

'My rakhi brother, you have to help out. My father and his men are now taking shelter at the mosque. You are a Mughal commander now in charge of law and order in Delhi. Your friend Ibrahim Hussain, who was with Raja Hemu, also joined the Mughal forces just before the war. Why don't you help me?'

'My sister, I will always be there for you, like I had promised on the very first day you walked into my house. Why do you worry? I will make arrangements.'

'Aditya, move the men in the mosque to Chanderi Mahal, the zenana under the control of my friend Ibrahim Hussian. The Mughal soldiers will not come searching the Mahal. I will ensure their safety. You move with your wife and mother, along with these men in your custody now. Move fast.'

Aditya moved quickly. All of them moved into Chanderi Mahal. They were all asked to stay in the underground apartment.

✺

80

The next day at Chanderi Mahal, Meera met her father.

'My daughter, you see the fate that has befallen us. I denounced you years ago. But now I am under the protection of your son, my grandson. My son Hemu's death was accidental, while Akbar's victory, providential. Had that treacherous Ramaiya's greed not intervened as an arrow, Raja Hemu would not have succumbed to any pressure. He won twenty-two wars in succession. He was an unconquered monarch. He was not killed in war, but murdered by cowards.'

'Father, please do not put so much strain on yourself. Whatever happened has happened. We should only look at what happens next. I could not talk to my brother Hemu. On the day of his coronation, I could only see him briefly. After that, quite a few unpleasant things happened. I hope he recovers and gets back to his glorious past. You rest now. Let us plan the next step,' Meera intervened.

Meanwhile, the sad news reached them. Pir Mohammad, a Mughal commander, had found Hemu in a cave in the forest. He had seized Hemu's elephant Hawai and carried Raja Hemu away to Akbar's camp. The half-conscious Raja Hemu was beheaded. It was said that Bairam Khan asked Akbar to slay Hemu and establish the right to the title of Ghazi or champion of faith. The young Akbar naturally obeyed the instructions of his guardian, smote Raja Hemu on the neck with his scimitar, and the bystanders finished off the victim.

Raja Hemu's head was sent to Kabul, while his body was placed in a gibbet outside the Purana Qila in Delhi.

This sad news upset the whole group assembled at Chanderi Mahal.

'Why do I need to live this long, to listen to all the cruelties faced by my son?' Raja Hemu's father was heartbroken. His daughter and grandson tried their best to console him.

Two days passed in mourning. Meanwhile, thousands of people were killed in Delhi as a genocide had been ordered by Bairam Khan. Delhi was turning into a place of terror, minarets were built from the skulls of the dead.

Akbar entered Delhi in triumph. The treasures of Raja Hemu were seized.

The men hiding at Chanderi Mahal did not know what would happen to them. At that crucial hour, Abdul Gafoor came up with a brilliant plan.

81

This was the plan unveiled by Abdul Gafoor for those who were sheltering in Chanderi Mahal.

'Everyone in the group, other than Meera, will move out from here. Meera is my rakhi sister and no one will look for her head. She is safe with me. The rest of you have to move through an underground tunnel that will quickly be created by Aditya from under this Mahal. That tunnel will take you to the forests located on the northern side of the city near Wazirabad on the west bank of the Yamuna. There, you will be received by my son Asif, Aditya's friend. You will then get a safe passage into Bundelkhand, where our associates will provide you shelter. You will be far away from the current bustle of Delhi. You can live safely there. After the winds of violence subside, I will ensure that Meera joins you. Aditya, start your job quickly. Everyone will move with you as you make the underground tunnel. You should all start tomorrow afternoon, as we cannot stay longer and take chances.

'Until then, all of you stay in these underground apartments. Don't come up and show your faces to the inmates here. I do not want information to leak out at any cost.

'Only Meera will come up and stay with us, conveying that business is going on as usual here.

'All of you note this. I am doing this favour only for my dearest sister, even at the cost of earning the wrath of my Mughal bosses. You are therefore requested not to discuss this with anyone even after you reach the destination safely. Otherwise, my family and Meera's life will be in danger. Understand?'

Saying this, Abdul Gafoor went up. Meera ensured that she fed her family with her own hands. Her father and her son were ecstatic when they ate from her hands.

The next afternoon, everyone started to move out as planned. Meera bid them adieu with tears in her eyes.

'I will join you soon,' she told her father and her son.

Meera stayed back. After a few days, she left with her daughter-in-law and her foster brother to go to their native place, Shamsabad, in the Punjab region. She was told she would join her son and father in a month's time, once they had settled down.

They reached their place and got down to business as usual. A few days later, Meera made kheer, her daughter-in-law's and her rakhi brother's favourite dish.

They enjoyed the nice dinner, along with the kheer made by Meera. She started the conversation after dinner with a startling question, 'My dear brother, why did you do this to me?'

'What?' the confused Abdul Gafoor asked her.

'I know everything, my brother. Sorry to have treated you better than my own brother, Raja Hemu. I overheard the conversation you had with my daughter-in-law, Komal, last night about what happened to my father and son. You thought I was asleep.

'They were received by Asif, whom I considered my own son, while he was growing up with Aditya. Hawai, Raja Hemu's elephant, earlier captured by the Mughal forces, received them with a garland.

'Aditya was placed in a specially decorated enclosure on top of Hawai. He was surprised to receive such a reception from his friend and schoolmate. Until then, everything had seemed normal to him.

'When both Aditya and Asif sat in the decorated enclosure, Asif suddenly beheaded Aditya using a dagger concealed in his dress. Aditya's head fell down from the top of the elephant. Tears rolled down the eyes of Hawai upon seeing Aditya's head falling down.

'The people who had accompanied Aditya were stunned.

'My father was asked, "If you convert to Islam now, we can proclaim that Raja Hemu's father himself has converted. That will frighten everyone around. If you do not do so, you will end up with the same fate as that of your grandson. This is my order."

'Asif was very firm in his statement.

'He said, "We know Aditya had special powers. That is why we conceived a plan in which he would create an underground tunnel under our supervision. Otherwise, he would have escaped from right under our nose. Once we got Aditya here, we did not want to do anything until we placed him on top of Hemu's elephant. He did not find anything fishy around him. We killed him when he was on top of the elephant. This was done to ensure that he did not get any special aid from the super powers he had with reference to land. Once he was dissociated from land and attacked in a space above land, he could not exercise any of his special powers. The plan worked. The poor fellow believed till the end that I was his friend. But how could I, serving Mughal forces, be kind to him? For us, religious duties take precedence over all relationships. Serving the Mughals is my religious duty, since the Mughal kingdom will very soon convert this land to Islam. Do you want the same fate as that of your grandson?"

"Whoever you are, I do not care. I lived eighty years praying to my God. Why should I change my God at this age when I am almost done with life?"

"You want to showcase me as a model for conversion to claim that even Raja Hemu's father converted to Islam. You want this message to go down all across this land, so that religious conversion can happen faster."

"I declare that I would prefer to die at your hands than change my religion. I am the father of the brave warrior Raja Hemu. Cut me into pieces. I am ready. Spread the message that the eighty-year-old father of Raja Hemu preferred death to loss of dignity. Go ahead with your mission. I am ready to accept death."

'The firmness of Raja Hemu's conviction was visible in his father's eyes. All the men, Hindus and Afghan Muslims, also acknowledged his commitment. All of them preferred death as the best way to protect their honour and dignity. They all shouted, "Long live Raja Hemu! Long live Raja Hemu!"

'Everyone was killed. A minaret was constructed with their heads, and their bodies thrown away into the Yamuna.

'Abdul Gafoor, you cheat. Don't think I don't know anything. Your bosses adopted hot pursuit and you adopted a soft approach. You wanted to destroy Hemu's family, some of them by cruel force and some of us by using a soft, cunning approach.

'You made me hate my brother, my husband and my daughter. I was almost convinced that the criticism of the hard conversion approach adopted by your rulers was overstated. That was your clever strategy.

'You wanted to hold us captive but disguised this efficiently by making us your permanent guests. You indirectly persuaded my son Aditya into joining Raja Hemu in the disguise of an Islamic person.

'You forced me to go to the coronation of Raja Hemu and give him a surprise, knowing full well that Hemu might dislike it. You created a situation by which he would denounce me and my son at a time when he needed my son as a crucial support. You gathered intelligence inputs from my son, when he was with Hemu. He never knew your intentions and discussed many of his plans with you, considering you his most reliable foster uncle.

'Not only this, I met my daughter at Chanderi Mahal, the harem of your friend. You did not know of my meeting with her. My son-in-law, who was emasculated and made an eunuch serving as a guard for the women, also met me there. None of you knew that both my daughter and son-in-law were working in the same place. You destroyed my daughter, you raped her the moment you arrived. She never knew your name. You hid your identity completely from her.

'But, as soon as she saw me with you, she alerted me to your evil deeds. But it was too late. I met her only after seeing off my son and his group. Otherwise I would have stopped them from leaving, according to your evil designs.

'She was forced to spy on her own uncle Hemu through her former husband, my son-in-law. You gave her a child, whom you never treated well.

'You made her a concubine, a courtesan for all your dignitaries. My daughter, a sweet beautiful flower, was destroyed by you.

'You made me hate my husband. I came to know he ran away from Chanderi to protect the idols worshipped since the ancient days of Prahalad. He later became a sleeper cell by concealing his identity as a mullah in a mosque. He gave precise intelligence inputs to my brother and served as a true patriotic citizen. My son told me all this without your knowledge. But my son never doubted you at the time of leaving Chanderi Mahal. He thought that you did not know about the sleeper cell status of my husband and he did not want you to know that.

'Even I will not disclose where he is located, because he will continue to perform his national duty in his disguised identity somewhere.

'All this, I understand. But I don't understand why my Brahmin daughter-in-law Komal went against her own husband Aditya. They loved each other and got married. But why did she turn against him? I cannot understand.'

She concluded her long speech. She got her answer soon.

༼༽

82

'I will tell you why,' Abdul Gafoor started.

'Now that you know so much, you may also know this, your daughter-in-law is not a Hindu in the first place. She is a Muslim by birth. During the First Battle of Panipat, your brother Hemu was supplying gunpowder, food grains and other items to Ibrahim Lodi. Emperor Babur wanted to plant a spy in his trader network to learn how the local sourcing was being done. He wanted to develop his supply network well before the war. He knew Hemu was a leading supplier to Ibrahim Lodi, his enemy.

'Hence, he planted Syed Ibrahim as a rival trader in Mewat, from where your brother operated. He was spying on Hemu's trade activities according to the instructions of Babur. Hemu somehow learnt of this and reported it to the then ruler, Ibrahim Lodi.

'Ibrahim Lodi's men killed Syed Ibrahim at the request of Hemu. Lodi wanted to kill the whole family of Syed Ibrahim, who was my brother. His wife was pregnant at the time. Meanwhile,

Babur conquered Delhi and became the emperor. During that time, my brother's wife died while delivering a baby girl at the Sufi centre, which referred you to me. The Sufi centre is a sleeper cell of the Mughals. It saved the baby girl.

'Fearing that the girl may be killed by Hemu, the Sufi saint sent her to Shamsabad to Bhagwan Das, the Bhakti movement priest, as a Brahmin orphan girl.

'Sufism and the Bhakti movement aligned with each other in many areas, as they promoted unity amongst Hindus and Muslims. But Bhagwan Das did not know that the Sufi centre was a sleeper cell of the Mughals.

'I ensured that the girl reached Bhagwan Das's house safely. He adopted her and brought her up as a Brahmin girl. She was a Muslim girl, my brother's daughter.

'The same Sufi saint spotted you at the slave market. He knew the entire family of Hemu and hence could easily identify you. He therefore referred you to me, so that we could hold you captive, but disguised as my genuine guest.

'You became victim to our plans. But we wanted to get precise intelligence on Hemu. How could we do that?

'I prompted my brother's daughter who also nourished her ambition of taking revenge on Hemu's family. I told her to love your son. He fell for her. I encouraged their love and later their marriage by convincing you.

'I made your daughter-in-law encourage her husband to go and join Hemu's forces. All plans fell into place.

'Now it is your turn to either die or be converted to Islam and become a preacher. The choice is yours,' Abdul Gafoor completed his story.

'Oh, you think you are deciding my fate. Who are you to decide? I have already decided, not only my fate, but yours as well.

'The kheer that I gave you had the most dangerous poison.

Both of you enjoyed eating it. Now you will both die soon. I will also join you in death, as I also ate it. When my son himself has died, why should I live? But I wanted to finish you before I left this world. My mission is accomplished.'

Meera loudly laughed. Both Abdul Gafoor and Komal were shocked.

'My son Aditya, you were born to a Brahmin pandit and a Vaishya mother. You were brought up by an Islamic family. You disguised yourself as a practising Muslim and served a Hindu commander, your uncle Raja Hemu. You married a Muslim girl disguised as a Brahmin girl. You were killed by your enemy disguised as your friend and brother.

'My son, your religious and caste identities were misplaced in this birth. After your death, your physical identity is not even traceable, as your head, along with those of many others, is in a minaret, while your body is in the Yamuna.

'I apologize for all this. I never knew such atrocities would happen to you. Had I known this, I would not have run away from the jauhar when I was carrying you.

'There is one thing I can say with confidence. In this Karmic avatar, you were operating with concealed identities. But to avenge these enemies, you will come back in a new avatar, wherein the enemy cannot see you while you wage war invisibly. I pray to the Almighty to grant you the boon to complete the unfinished task assigned to you by your uncle, Raja Hemu.

'The Hindu Rashtra of Raja Hemu, which was created a month ago, has crumbled and the Mughal empire has begun its full-fledged journey in our Bharat. Paradoxically, both Hindus and Afghan Muslims were killed by the Mughals.

'In spite of the severe atrocities faced by the Hindu community, there were still some sensible people from both religions who cared for people across all religions in the Hindu Rashtra of Raja Hemu.

Humanity could still be seen amongst people from both religions, even in the middle of the worst bloodbath our land has known.

'Let my son be reborn and create a secular Raj where all religious communities co-exist peacefully. This is the last wish of my brother, Raja Hemu, and also his beloved sister, this Meera.'

Uttering these emotional words, she fell dead along with Abdul Gafoor and Komal.

While this tragedy was unfolding, her daughter Heera was entertaining the audience at Chanderi Mahal with her song, composed by Kabir.

Ud Jayega Huns Akela
Jug Darshan ka Mela
Jaise Paat Gire Taruvar se,
Milna Bahut Duhela
Naa Jane kidhar Girega
Layega Pawan ka Rela
Jub Hone Umur Puri,
Jab Chutega Hukum Huzuri
Jum ke Doot Bade Mazboot
Jum se Pada Jhamela...

The swan will fly away all alone,
The spectacle of the world will be a mere fair
As the leaf falls from the tree
It is difficult to find
Who knows where it will fall
Once it is struck by a gust of wind.
When life is complete
Listening to orders, following
others will end...

The Mughal nobles were enthralled by her performance.

But Heera was thinking about her two sons, one born out of wedlock and another born of service as a concubine of a Mughal commander. She looked up, praying to the Almighty to let her sons breathe the air of liberty and freedom some day in future.

Would they...?

Epilogue

Before Aditya's soul departed, it had a great vision for the future of Bharat. He dreamt of a unified Bharat focusing on the development of all, torture and appeasement of none and an egalitarian society with fairness for all. He believed that the future Bharat should be headed by a leader like Raja Hemu, who rose from a poor background to become an emperor, a leader who considers performance-based metrics the sole criteria of governance.

With these dreams, Aditya's soul departed and moved on to its next Karmic journey. Aditya's head became invisible amongst the many heads hanging on the pillar.

But his departed soul started its war invisibly as 'The Guerilla Warrior' in the era of Maha Rana Pratap Singh, in his next Karmic journey.

The forthcoming release *The Guerilla Warrior* will tell you about his next Karmic journey and his unique approach to wars.

∽

Acknowledgements

At the outset, I have to thank the Almighty for kindling my passion to write. What did not occur to me in the past few decades suddenly arose in my mind as a spark one morning. That spark has lit flames of unbridled passion in me.

I register my gratitude to my think tank. Its dynamic members, with their youth and exuberance, tolerated my constant intrusion into their personal time. They supported me in perfecting the core story design, ensuring the smooth flow of the narrative and promoting the book.

The key members of this think tank, who walked along with me shoulder to shoulder on this project, are Padmanabh Diwanji (Paddy) from UAE, Priyanka Durgadoss and Jyothsna Durgadoss from California.

There were others that relentlessly assisted me in terms of the research, conversion of manuscripts into digital files and fulfilling the role of critics. They include Vijayakumaran (UAE) and Vijoy Joseph (UAE).

I am grateful to the Rupa team for showing confidence in this book and taking the series forward. The assistance we got from them was invaluable. The team has worked hard to polish the manuscript and get it to the publication stage.

I would like to register my gratitude to Madhav Menon (UAE), whose enthusiastic guidance from day one helped convert my dream into reality. He was instrumental in helping me reach the right publisher.

Above all, I could not have spent quality time on this project but for the support of my wife Gowri Durgadoss.

Further, I thank all those who follow me on Facebook, Twitter, YouTube, Google Plus, Instagram, my blogs and my website.

The book relies on a vast body of research by a large number of scholars. I thank all these sources and have cited them wherever possible.

Finally, I register my debt of gratitude to all my well-wishers.

I am happy to welcome the enthusiastic new young member of the think tank, Vivek Venkatraghvan.

My special thanks to my media partners who tirelessly connect me to readers through social media platforms 24/7: Lakshmi Narasimhan V.B., www.jackofclicks.com and Vinit Madavan. I also thank the promotion and distribution team of my publishers.